Adaptation and abridgment by Alissa Heyman
Original Spanish text adapted by Manuel Serrat Crespo and Ferran Alexandri
Illustrations by Pedro Rodríguez

Library of Congress Cataloging-in-Publication Data available

STERLING and the distinctive Sterling logo are registered trademarks of
Sterling Publishing Co., Inc.

10 9 8 7 6 5 4 3 2 1

Published in 2008 by Sterling Publishing Co., Inc.
387 Park Avenue South, New York, NY 10016
© 2006 Parramón Ediciones, S.A.
Originally published in Spain under the title El Gran Libro de las Aventuras
English translation and abridgment copyright © 2008 by Sterling Publishing Co., Inc.

Distributed in Canada by Sterling Publishing
c/o Canadian Manda Group, 165 Dufferin Street
Toronto, Ontario, Canada M6K 3H6
Distributed in the United Kingdom by GMC Distribution Services
Castle Place, 166 High Street, Lewes, East Sussex, England BN7 1XU
Distributed in Australia by Capricorn Link (Australia) Pty. Ltd.
P.O. Box 704, Windsor, NSW 2756, Australia

Manufactured in China
All rights reserved

Sterling ISBN: 978-1-4027-5156-1

For information about custom editions, special sales, premium and
corporate purchases, pleasecontact Sterling Special Sales
Department at 800-805-5489 or specialsales@sterlingpub.com

THE BIG BOOK OF ADVENTURE

Illustrated by
PEDRO RODRÍGUEZ

Abridged and Adapted by Alissa Heyman

STERLING

New York / London
www.sterlingpublishing.com/kids

Contents

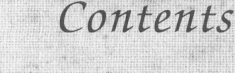

1660(?)-1731

Daniel Defoe

Daniel Defoe was a famous English novelist, journalist, merchant, and spy. He is most remembered for writing the adventure novel *Robinson Crusoe*. Born Daniel Foe, he added the "De" to his last name to make it sound more aristocratic—his father had been a working-class candle maker.

Written in 1719, *Robinson Crusoe* is considered by many to be the first English novel. The book is based on the true story of a Scottish sailor, Alexander Selkirk, who was shipwrecked on a desert island for many years.

Defoe was a very prolific writer, and sometimes his writing got him in trouble. A satirical pamphlet he wrote in praise of religious tolerance was misunderstood and led to his imprisonment. He was released in exchange for becoming a spy. Acting as a secret agent for the English government, Defoe helped bring about a treaty between Scotland and England in 1707.

Defoe also wrote the novels *Moll Flanders*, *A Journal of the Plague Year*, and two sequels to *Robinson Crusoe*. Defoe helped make the novel popular in England.

ROBINSON CRUSOE

My Early Adventures

I was born in 1632 in the English city of York. My mother belonged to a good English family, and my father was a wealthy German merchant. He wanted me to be a lawyer, but I desired nothing more than to sail the seas and wander the world. My father disapproved, warning me that I was not born for a great life, and that kings themselves would envy the happiness of an ordinary life. Despite my father's commands, when I was nineteen I disobeyed him and ran away from home. There was something in my nature that made me ignore my family's wishes, leading to my future life of hardship and misery.

Without asking God or my father's blessing, I joined a friend on a voyage to London. While sailing we hit a terrible storm. I was sick and scared. It was only by a miracle that our crew was rescued by another boat. As our ship sank I could scarcely look at it, for my heart felt dead with fright, and I was filled with horror at the thought that I had almost drowned. Reason told me I should go back home, that this was a sign I was not meant for life at sea, but I was stubborn.

I set out on a voyage to the coast of Africa. This trip also met with misfortune. Near the Canary Islands, a Turkish pirate ship chased us and our entire crew was taken prisoner. The pirates took us to a port in Northern Africa where the captain kept me as a prize, making me his slave.

For two years I thought of nothing but escape. One day when I was with a relative of the pirate captain and another slave, Xury, I saw the chance I had been waiting for. At sea in a fishing boat I was able to throw the captain's relative overboard.

I said to Xury, "If you wish to be loyal to me, I'll make a great man of you. If not, I'll throw you into the sea, too." The boy swore to be loyal and go all over the world with me.

We sailed for many days, fearful of being taken prisoner again. One day Xury sighted a Portuguese sailing ship, and we sailed out to meet it. I told the sailors that I was an Englishman who had escaped from pirates, and they agreed to help us. We set our course for Brazil, and when we got there the Portuguese captain was very generous. He gave me good money for my boat. In addition, he recommended me to a landowner who had a sugar plantation. I then learned the process of making sugar and bought some land. Although at first it only provided me with enough to keep me alive, in time my business grew and brought me wealth.

I could have stayed in Brazil, comfortably leading the kind of life my father wanted for me. But again, I was the willful agent of my own misery. Longing immodestly to rise faster in the world, I could not resist a proposal to travel to Guinea in search of slaves to work my plantation. I rashly sailed from Brazil, leaving my lands in the care of friends and designating the Portuguese captain who had saved me as my sole heir. My father's good counsel was again lost upon me.

At first the weather was calm, but later a terrible hurricane threw us off course. We no longer knew where we were. The storm had carried us far from any shipping route.

Finally the ship ran aground. Desperately we pushed a small boat into the water and those of us still alive climbed into it, although the sea was so wild we believed we were heading for our own execution. As we came closer to shore the land looked more frightful than the sea. Then a raging, mountainlike wave broke against our little craft and swallowed us up. I sank into the sea and was buried in water. Struggling for air, another gigantic wave swept me up and carried me half dead to the beach. I managed to clamber up the cliffs of the shore, finally out of reach of the furious waves.

The Island

Safe on shore, I gave thanks to God for saving me, reflecting that all my companions must have drowned. Soaked to the skin and without anything or anyone but a dog and two cats that had escaped from the ship, all I could expect was to die of hunger or to be devoured by wild beasts. For a while, I ran around like a madman. Then I thought about how best to survive and climbed in a tree for the night to wait out the storm.

Next morning the weather was clear, and I could see that the waves had pushed the ship against the rocks about a mile from where I was. I swam out to the boat to get provisions and found that the food had remained miraculously dry. Seeing that I could recover a number of tools in addition to food and drink, I built a raft of logs and loaded it with everything I could: bread, rice, cheese, dried meats, grain, and bottles of liquor. I also took tools to work the land, a carpenter's toolbox, firearms, ammunition, and two barrels of gunpowder. With difficulty, I steered my raft to the coast. I returned to the ship eleven times, but on the twelfth day, after another storm, the ship had disappeared.

After about twelve days I realized that I would soon lose track of time. To prevent this, I drove a large post into the beach where I first landed, and with a knife, carved on it the date of my arrival—30TH OF SEPTEMBER, 1659. Every day I carved a new line on the post, and thus I kept my calendar.

My next work was to view my new country. I did not know if I was on an island or a continent, if it was deserted or inhabited. But my doubts disappeared when, from the top of a hill, I saw that the land was completely surrounded by water and that there was no other land in sight aside from some distant islets. At that moment I cried, reflecting that I would die in this desolate place.

My Castle

I explored the island, looking for a place to live that would be near fresh water, shelter me from the sun, and offer safety from wild beasts. I finally decided to make my home in a little plain, next to a steep, rocky hill. I drew a semicircle on the earth and set up two rows of stout posts to form a protective fence.

Within the fence—my fortress—I placed all my possessions and raised a big tent made from the ship's sails to shelter me from the rain. At the back of the tent, there was a hollow in the rock that I enlarged into a cave and used as my storeroom.

I did not build a door in the fortress, but instead used a ladder that could be taken up at night. The lack of proper tools made my work slow and wearisome; it took me close to a year to complete the job. Once it was done, I called the place my castle.

While working, tears often came to my eyes and I would lose all hope. But then I remembered that though I was in despair, I was lucky to still be alive. I began to try to improve my way of life by reading the Bible and making furniture. I also began to write a journal, which lasted until my supply of ink ran out.

September 30, 1659

I, poor, wretched Robinson Crusoe, having been shipwrecked in a terrible storm, reached this island, which I call the Island of Despair. The entire crew has died and only I was saved. I did not have . . .

Life on the Island

My daily life was very ordered. Every morning, unless it was raining, I would go out hunting. I discovered the presence of wild goats, and I lived on these animals for some time. Then I worked until mid-morning. Afterward I ate and rested for a good while, and then in the afternoon I set to work again.

I had saved some shoots of barley and rice that I had found on the ship and that had amazingly sprouted. I managed to discover the best times of year for planting, and in time I came to harvest big crops. I had a good store of rice and barley grain. I learned to make plates, containers, and pitchers out of clay, and, with more work, I built an oven and succeeded in making bread. After a few years on the island, I had managed to live with a certain amount of comfort.

New Horizons

During my fourth year on the island, I built a large canoe to sail close to shore. One day the current carried me out to sea, and it required a great effort to get back to land. When I reached my castle, I went to sleep and awoke to someone calling me, "Robin, poor Robinson Crusoe! Where have you been?" It was my parrot, Poll, who I had taught to say a few words.

I began to set traps to catch the wild goats so I could tame and raise them. I eventually achieved my purpose and managed to assemble a good-size flock. I now had meat whenever I wanted, and milk, too, from which I could make butter and cheese.

I no longer felt desperate to escape. The civilized world seemed remote from my existence, and I was glad to be free from man's wickedness. I no longer cared about money and profit. I had enough to eat and supply my wants. What was all the rest to me?

A Footprint in the Sand

After eighteen years on the island, one morning when I was going to my canoe I found to my great surprise the print of a man's naked foot in the sand. I stood thunderstruck, as if I had seen a ghost. I looked around in every direction. I climbed to the top of a hill but saw no one and so returned to the castle, deeply scared and imagining a man was following me.

That night I could not sleep. Had human beings arrived here? Were they savages? Had they come to devour me? Wild fancies filled my imagination and I did not dare leave my fortress.

I finally got the nerve to explore—perhaps the print was just my own!—but I discovered that at the tip of the island where I had never been before, there was a beach covered with skulls, hands, feet, and other human bones. There were also the remains of a great bonfire where cannibals must have feasted upon their prisoners.

Horrified by the sight of such brutality, I became so afraid that I decided to build another fortification for my castle. I positioned my guns so that I could quickly fire all my artillery. I planted thick trees outside the enclosure, and in six years my fortress was impenetrable.

I knew that I might well spend another eighteen years without seeing anyone, but still I shut myself up within my fortress for two years. Night and day I thought about how I might destroy the monsters at their bloody entertainment and, if possible, rescue their victims

I found a place to hide and watch for the cannibals to come to shore. One morning, after twenty-three years on the island, I saw the light of a fire on the beach. I was overcome with terror. I threw myself to the ground and through my telescope I saw nine naked savages dancing around a bonfire.

Friday

The savages left in their canoes. More than two years later more came, about thirty men. They brought with them two prisoners and, throwing one of them to the ground next to their fire, they began to cut him to pieces. The other victim managed to flee and came running down the beach, straight toward me. Two men began to chase him, but the fugitive was far ahead of them. I decided the time had come for me to have a servant and that I had to save the poor creature's life. I shot and killed his pursuers, freeing him. I smiled encouragingly and called to the fugitive, who after hesitation, fell to his knees before me and kissed the ground to show his gratitude.

He was a young, handsome fellow, and after giving him food and drink, he slept. In a short time I began to teach him to speak my language, and the first words I said to him were, "You will be called Friday, because that was the day I saved your life."

I taught him my name and how to say yes and no. I gave him clothing. He learned quickly how to do the things I taught him and worked hard in the fields. I was delighted with my new companion. My life became so pleasant that if there had been no threat from cannibals I would have been completely content.

I taught Friday how to be a good Christian, and he began to speak English quite well. Friday told me that our island was in the mouth of the Orinoco River and that we were near the big island of Trinidad. We spent three very pleasant years together.

In my twenty-seventh year on the island, twenty-one more savages arrived with two prisoners, one of whom was a white man, bound hand and foot. Friday and I began to fire our muskets, killing and wounding as many cannibals as we could. The rest ran off to their canoes. I untied the prisoner, who turned out to be a Spaniard. The other victim was also tied up. I set him free and told Friday to talk to him, but he could not do so because he began to cry and kiss him—the man was Friday's father!

My island was now peopled, and I saw myself as a king rich with subjects.

Return

We no longer had to fear cannibals. If they returned, we could fight them. Thus we went freely all over the island. But still, the idea of escape was never far from my thoughts.

One day Friday came running and told me of the arrival of a vessel. I saw it was an English ship that had dropped anchor. I was suspicious. A small boat was approaching with eight men who appeared to be bringing three prisoners with them. It appeared to be bringing three prisoners with them. As I watched, the men abandoned the captives on the beach and rowed away. I greeted the three captives. When they recovered from the shock of hearing English, I learned that they were the captain of the ship, his second in command, and a passenger, and that they had been victims of a mutiny among the crew.

Through trickery and confusion Friday and I managed to subdue the mutineers. We took back the ship from them and I obtained from the captain a promise to take me back to England free of charge. Friday accompanied me.

And so it was that I left that island after having lived there for twenty-eight years. I reached England after an absence of thirty-five years and found that almost all my family had died. The money I had was not enough to allow me to settle down, so Friday and I embarked for Portugal. There my old friend the Portuguese captain gave me the news that I had a fruitful sugar plantation in Brazil.

I sold the plantation for a good sum of money and settled in England. I married and had three children, but as the years passed my wanderer's heart began to beat again. I knew I would set sail once more, looking for new adventures.

1828-1905

Jules Verne

Jules Verne was a French author of adventure novels who drew upon his interest in science and geography to write about space, air, and underwater travel. He is best known for his novels *Journey to the Center of the Earth*, *Around the World in Eighty Days*, and *Twenty Thousand Leagues Under the Sea*. He also helped pioneer the genre of science fiction, along with the British author H. G. Wells.

Born in Nantes, France, he summered with his family near the Loire River where he and his brother would often rent boats and where the many ships navigating the river sparked Verne's imagination. As a child he became very interested in exploration.

Verne went to Paris to study law but dropped law for writing. His father found out and withdrew financial support. Verne had to make money by selling his stories and by working as a stockbroker (which he hated doing). While in Paris he met the famous French novelists Alexandre Dumas and Victor Hugo.

Jules Verne anticipated many scientific achievements of the twentieth century. He wrote more than fifty books during his lifetime, and many plays and films have been made from his widely read works.

JOURNEY TO THE CENTER OF THE EARTH

The Mysterious Parchment

One Sunday my German uncle, Professor Otto Lidenbrock, came rushing back to his house. He was heading for his study when he shouted, "Follow me, Axel!"

My uncle was a professor of philosophy, chemistry, geology, and mineralogy. He was a great scientist, capable of classifying any mineral among the six hundred known types. And I, his orphaned nephew, who loved mineralogy above all else, had become an assistant to this brilliant but impatient man.

My uncle was absorbed in an old book. "A masterpiece! This is the chronicle of the Norwegian princes who ruled Iceland! A manuscript dating from the twelfth century!"

A small scrap of parchment fell out of the book. My uncle grabbed it, and, as he spread it flat on the table, we could discern some letters of an old, magical text that my uncle said was ancient runic script. He saw at once that there was a secret in those symbols and determined to discover it. He began to transcribe each character using the letters of our alphabet, but all that appeared was a list of words without meaning.

"It's a code," he cried, striking the table with his fist. "Someone hid a message in these letters. Undoubtedly it conceals the key to a great discovery!"

On the second page of the book there was a note, perhaps by the same person who had written the parchment. All that could be read was "Arne Saknussemm," the name of a celebrated Icelandic scholar and alchemist from the sixteenth century.

My uncle declared he wouldn't eat or sleep until he had discovered the secret—and informed me that I wouldn't either.

Since I would eventually want to eat and sleep, I also tried to decipher the message. To my surprise, when it was written backward I found the words *crater* and *Earth*. Then it came upon me like a flash of lightning. I had got the clue! You could read the entire text backward. I was terrified—a man had had the courage to penetrate the center of the Earth. . .

I turned to my uncle, saying, "I have made a very important discovery."

His eyes flashed with excitement. "You don't mean to say that you have any idea of the meaning of the scrawl?"

"I do. It means nothing if you read from left to right, but if from right to left—"

"Backward!" cried my uncle in amazement. "Oh most cunning Saknussemm!"

He snatched up the document and began to read:

Bold traveler: descend by way of the crater at Sneffels glacier that the shadow of Scartaris touches before the end of June and you will reach the center of the Earth. I did it.
Arne Saknussemm

My uncle leaped three feet from the ground with joy. "Axel, pack your bag and mine!"

The Bold Journey Begins

A chill went down my spine on hearing these words. To go to the center of the Earth! What madness! I wanted to make my uncle see that it was all nonsense—a hoax. Besides, what was the meaning of those words—*Sneffels* and *Scartaris*—that I had never heard in my life?

"Very simple," my uncle said. "Look at this map of Iceland. The whole island is composed of volcanoes. If we follow the coast to this peninsula, we come to a mountain. That's Sneffels, an extinct volcano, made up of several craters. Toward the end of June, Scartaris, one of the mountain peaks, must throw its shadow precisely on the crater that leads to the center of the Earth."

"Well," I cried, overcome at last, "let us go and see!"

"Fear nothing and say not a word to any living soul. Our success depends on secrecy and speed."

I left my uncle's study. Our preparations were soon done, and we departed even sooner than expected on our journey into the center of the Earth.

Hans, Our Icelandic Guide

We reached Copenhagen at the beginning of June and then embarked for Iceland, one of the largest islands in Europe, on the ship *Valkyrie*. When we reached the bay of Reykjavík my uncle pointed to a mountain with two peaks.

"Sneffels!" he exclaimed.

The first thing we did was to hire a guide to accompany us on our climb up the extinct volcano. Hans was a tall, powerful man with intelligent eyes and an innocent expression. He was a duck hunter and did not talk much.

Then we began to make our final preparations. In addition to a thermometer, a stopwatch, two compasses, and a number of lanterns, we took picks, walking sticks, ladders, and ropes. We took enough meat and biscuits for six months.

We traveled for days. We reached land that seemed crushed under the weight of enormous stones. Finally we saw the immense base of the volcano. Sneffels is almost 5,000 feet tall. I was frightened at the thought of the volcano erupting, but my uncle again assured me that it was quite safe. I wasn't so sure.

To the Earth's Center

Climbing the mountainside was very difficult. Only Hans's skill kept us from being crushed on rocks below. I never felt such exhaustion in my life. I was ready to faint from hunger and cold. At last we reached the summit of Sneffels. It was a wondrous sight.

We ate and rested, and then began the climb down the volcano. At midday we reached the bottom. Sneffels was composed of three chimneys, which when it was active would have poured forth burning lava and poisonous vapors. The professor examined each chimney thoroughly. Suddenly he gave a wild cry.

"Axel!" he shouted. "Come here—it's wonderful!"

With great joy he read an inscription on the block of stone: ARNE SAKNUSSEMM.

"Now, unbeliever, do you begin to have faith?" cried my uncle.

We were at the end of June and had only to wait for the shadow of Scartaris to point the way, just as the text written by the Icelandic wise man said. And after several cloudy days the sun finally indicated the central chimney. "There it is!" said the professor. "Now our journey really begins!"

Was this the last I should ever see of any sky? I looked down the horrible abyss and my hair stood up on end. It was like a gaping well, with walls that ran straight up and down. My uncle slipped one half of a rope around an outcropping rock and let the other half fall toward the bottom. In this way, holding tight to the two halves we could descend and then recover the rope when we got to the bottom. Loaded down with our baggage, we went down in this order: Hans, my uncle, and I. After ten and a half hours of exhausting descent, we reached the bottom of the chimney, where we could finally rest.

We turned on our lanterns and the effect was magical! "Forward!" cried my uncle, and we were engulfed in the dismal passage. We moved forward with our lanterns, along slopes covered with hardened lava of an infinite variety of colors.

According to the professor's calculations we were now well below sea level—a depth that had never before been reached.

Here I pointed out to my uncle our greatest danger: lack of water.

Rationing our water carefully, for days we went down farther and farther until we reached a crossroads from which there emerged two narrow, dark paths. My uncle chose the tunnel that had the steepest incline. After a while, I realized that we were going up. We had taken the wrong road!

Without Water

We turned back and retraced our steps. Unless we found water soon we would die of thirst. The sufferings we endured were horrible. My uncle led us on until my limbs refused to carry me farther. My eyes could no longer see. My knees shook. I gave one despairing cry and fell.

"Help, I am dying!" The last thing I saw was my uncle's face distorted with sorrow and then my eyes closed.

When I regained consciousness I saw Hans leaving us. During a long, weary hour delirious thoughts came to my mind, all sorts of reasons as to why our faithful guide had departed. Suddenly, however, there arose, as it were from the depths of the earth, a voice of comfort. Hans appeared, saying "*Vatten.*"

"Water! Water," I cried, waking up my uncle. We followed Hans as he led us down the tunnel. An hour later we had advanced a thousand yards and descended two thousand feet. At that moment I heard a well-known sound running along the floors of the granite rock—a kind of dull and sullen roar, like that of a distant waterfall.

"There's no doubt about it," the professor said excitedly, "an underground river is flowing beside us." With a pick Hans began to cut through the rock little by little, until a whistling was heard and a gush of water came out. I plunged my hands into the jet and immediately shouted, "It's boiling!" But at least we had water—we would wait until it cooled off. We would survive!

Lost!

A terrible incident happened to me on the 7th of August when I was walking first in line, followed by my companions. I was examining different layers of granite and was completely absorbed in my work. When I halted and turned around, I found that I was alone!

I turned back and shouted, but there was no one. I ascended the tunnel for over half an hour, hearing only the echoes of my own footsteps. At last I stopped. My lantern went out and I was left in darkness. I was literally buried alive! No words can depict my utter despair. I was lost, lost, LOST!

I started shouting, running, but eventually lost my strength. I fell and lost consciousness.

When I awoke I was bleeding from my fall. Suddenly I heard a sound, then nothing. It seemed like voices in the distance. I shouted with all my strength.

"Uncle Lidenbrock!"

"Axel! Is it you? Where are you?" responded a faraway voice.

"Lost and with no light."

"Axel," I heard my uncle say, "you got lost in one of the many passages that lead to the big cavern where we are. All you have to do is crawl downward and you'll find us."

So I started dragging myself along until I fell into a hole. When I reached the bottom, I hit it so hard that I lost consciousness again. When I recovered my senses, I found myself with my head bandaged and wrapped in blankets, with Hans and my uncle looking down at me.

"He's alive!"

I felt very weak. There were no lamps or torches lit, but an unexplainable light came in through an opening in the cave. "Have we gone back to the surface, Uncle Lidenbrock?"

"Of course not! Now rest and tomorrow we shall go on board."

On board what—and how?

The Lidenbrock Sea

At first I could see nothing, but when my eyes got used to the light I was astonished. "The sea!"

"Yes," replied my uncle with pride. "No future navigator will deny the fact of my having discovered it."

It was quite true. We were in front of a vast expanse of water. A sea in the middle of the Earth! The beach, the waves, everything was just like an earthly sea—only horribly savage. The shore consisted of golden sand and small shells. An unknown light acted as a sun and lit up the cave. Yet it was not like the sun, for it gave no heat. After so many days in those dark tunnels it was marvelous, yet sad. Instead of sky above, there was only a heavy roof of granite. We called it the Lidenbrock Sea, in honor of the professor.

When I got my strength back, we walked along the beach and discovered an amazing landscape. Behind a hill there was a lofty forest with trees that seemed like umbrellas. As we came closer we saw the trees were actually giant mush-rooms! Then we came upon flowering ferns as tall as pine trees. And on the ground we found a jawbone, then a whole skeleton. Here were the bones of mastodons—prehistoric elephants long extinct!

My uncle wanted to travel to the far shore, so Hans built a raft. We set out to sea. We sailed rapidly, far beyond anything possible on the Earth's surface. Before us was nothing but the vast and apparently limitless ocean, which must have been as wide as the Mediterranean or even the great Atlantic Ocean. We sailed for days, finally catching a living fish with no eyes—a species long extinct on Earth. We lowered an iron bar into the ocean to test the water's depth, and when we pulled it out we found it crushed by giant teeth marks! I was terrified by the thought of an enormous unknown monster.

Suddenly we came upon a huge sea lizard, a forty-foot turtle, and a whale. Hans seized the rudder to escape when a giant crocodile and a sea serpent came on either side of us. The rest of the fearful creatures plunged beneath the waves as those two monsters passed within fifty feet of the raft, and then made a rush at one another—their fury preventing them from seeing us. A deadly struggle commenced. We distinctly made out every action of the two hideous monsters, each who wanted to be sole king of the seas. They raised mountains of water, which dashed in spray over the raft. We seemed on the point of being upset and hurled headlong into the waves when the opponents drew away from us and disappeared beneath the waves.

Suddenly, at no great distance from us, an enormous mass rose out of the waters—the serpent was wounded, twisting and curling in the agony of death. At last the body of the mighty snake lay unmoving on the surface of the now calm waters.

Later a big storm broke and a hurricane pushed us along at incredible speed. Lightning flashed and thunder roared as if the world were about to explode. After many days the raft was cast upon the rocky shore. According to the calculations of the professor, we had traveled the entire length of Europe. But when my uncle excitedly consulted the compass he realized we had returned to the shore we had started out from.

Saknussemm's Sign

There could be no doubt about it, unwelcome as was the fact. During the tempest, there had been a change in the direction of the wind, and thus the raft had carried us back to the shores we had left so many days before!

We walked down the beach until we found a dagger and two letters half erased at the entrance of a dark, gloomy tunnel.

"A.S.!" my uncle exclaimed. "Arne Saknussemm! We're on the right track!"

Blessings on the storm! It brought us safely back to the very spot from which fine weather would have driven us forever. We went into the tunnel but were soon stopped by an immense block of granite. How had Saknussemm got through there? Perhaps a rock slide had covered the entrance. We made a desperate decision to blow it up with gunpowder.

The explosion caused the ground below us to crack. A dark abyss opened and started swallowing up the sea. The draining water was pulling our raft at great speed along a wide tunnel. Hans managed to light the lantern, and we saw that all our cargo had disappeared. We now had no food! Soon after, the light from the lantern went out. The steep incline of the waters was too much. We were falling!

Going Upward

Suddenly I noted that our raft was hitting against something that was not a solid body. What could it be?

"We're going up a waterspout!" my uncle exclaimed.

As we went up I touched the wall. "It's burning!" Then I touched the water that was pushing us upward. "It's boiling!" A terrible fear gripped me. I looked at the compass. It had gone mad!

"Uncle, we're finished—walls that are moving, unbearable heat, the water boiling, the compass gone crazy. It's an earthquake!"

"No, Axel. I am expecting something far more important. We are in the chimney of a volcano in eruption."

"What? We're going to be thrown out with the boiling lava and the flames?" I screamed.

"Yes," the professor calmly answered. "It's the only way to escape from the Earth's interior. The lava paste is heaving us up. Luckily we are inside a chimney of the volcano, not the main tunnel filled by burning lava."

We spent the whole night ascending, and finally we were cast out of the top of the volcano. When I opened my eyes again I was lying on a mountainside.

We climbed down the mountain, avoiding the lava flows. We came upon fields of olive and pomegranate trees and grapevines. Finding a spring, we quenched our thirst and ate pomegranates fresh from the vine. A little child appeared and my uncle asked him the name of the mountain in German, in English, and finally in Italian. The child answered, "Stromboli." We were on the Italian island of Sicily in the center of the Mediterranean! Entering one volcano, we had come out by way of another.

Home

We returned to Germany, reaching Hamburg on September 9th. There my uncle became a great man, and I, the nephew of a great man. My uncle enjoyed all the glory he deserved. I am informed that he is even to be seen made out of wax at Madame Tussaud's famous museum!

1812-1870

Charles Dickens

Charles Dickens (his full name was Charles John Huffan Dickens, penname "Boz") is considered the most important English novelist of the Victorian era and one of the greatest writers of the English language. Acclaimed worldwide for his memorable characters and rich storytelling, he is especially noted for novels such as *David Copperfield, Great Expectations, Oliver Twist, Bleak House,* and *A Christmas Carol.*

David Copperfield was first published as a serialized novel, meaning that the story appeared in installments every week or month in a popular journal. This kept the public anticipating each new part of the story. (It also meant that Dickens's novels were very long, since he got paid by the word!)

David Copperfield is fiction, but it draws on many of Dickens's personal experiences. Like David Copperfield, Dickens had an idyllic childhood until the age of twelve when his father lost money and had to go into prison for debt. To help the family make money, Dickens left school and began working ten-hour days in a bootblacking factory. This made Dickens a strong critic of the Victorian class and economic system.

DAVID COPPERFIELD

My World Falls Apart

I was born in Suffolk six months after my father died. On the day of my birth, my father's sister, Aunt Betsey, marched in and ordered my mother to give birth to a girl. When Aunt Betsey learned that I was a boy, she refused to have anything to do with me and stormed out of the house, never to return.

But my own first memories are full of the warm presence of my young mother, a beautiful, gentle woman. Unfortunately, she was not a strong person. She was vain and easily flattered, as an innocent child would be. When I recall those marvelous twelve years, neither can I forget the affection of Peggotty, the servant woman who took care of me and made me feel safe and loved.

But my world fell apart when Mr. Murdstone, a large man with black whiskers (he looked like a big, fierce dog!), appeared in my mother's life. That brutal man hid his cruelty under the disguise of firmness. He took absolute control of my mother's will. They were married while I was away on a trip with Peggotty.

Everything changed when Mr. Murdstone became my stepfather. He brought his worthless sister, Miss Jane Murdstone (whose eyebrows almost came together over the bridge of her nose), to help with the house. When my mother protested that she could run her own house, he threatened her into submission. He beat me when I couldn't remember my lessons. Nothing that I did seemed right, and a thousand times I ended up crying after Mr. and Miss Murdstone had punished me. I longed for my mother's embraces and Peggotty's good cheer from the time before those two monsters entered our lives.

Boarding School

My stepfather made the decision to send me to a boarding school when I bit his hand in self-defense during a savage beating with a cane after a particularly bad lesson. He was clever enough to convince my mother, who did not want to be separated from me, that I was wicked and needed more disciplining.

And so it was that I arrived at the desolate Salem House where I was forced to wear a sign that read, TAKE CARE. HE BITES. There I met the tyrannical headmaster Mr. Creakle, who never raised his voice above a fierce whisper and who would beat me with a cane. Far from my mother, living in a place totally unfamiliar to me, my first term at that boarding school would have been unbearable without the friendship of the confident, wealthy Steerforth, who was my protector (I called him "sir") and the loyal, kind Traddles, who drew little skeletons on his slate to cheer himself up after being beaten.

The highlight of my time at Salem House was when I got to go home for the holidays and spend a day with my mother, her new baby, and Peggotty without the Murdstones. I could see that my mother was thin and anxious and seemed almost brainwashed by the Murdstones, but still she lavished me with attention. As soon as the Murdstones returned I wasn't allowed to touch my baby brother and I was constantly criticized. I was almost glad to go back to boarding school.

When my birthday arrived, I was given the worst news of my life—my mother was dead and so was my baby brother.

I left Salem House the next day in a daze of grief. I didn't know that I would never return to the boarding school again and that another miserable period of my existence was about to begin.

From London to Dover

Miss Murdstone fired Peggotty and my stepfather got rid of me. He sent me to London to perform the very lowest tasks in the factory of Murdstone & Grinby. I was paid terribly and surrounded by coarse, uneducated people. I wondered what they thought of me eating my bread alone.

At least I had the good fortune to meet the shabby but talkative and genteel Mr. Micawber and his family, who were often a great consolation to me. Mr. Micawber never had any money. He went to debtor's prison yet always remained lively and cheerful. He helped keep my spirits up.

But when the Micawber family left London, things became unbearable. I decided to run away and find my Aunt Betsey Trotwood—the very same aunt who I had offended on the very day I was born without having the least responsibility for it. I hoped my aunt would forgive me for being a boy.

I got Aunt Betsey's address from Peggotty and set out for her house in Dover on foot. Exhausted and almost collapsing, I began to curse myself for my foolishness. When I passed by a used clothing shop in one town and saw feeble candles burning and trousers hanging like corpses, I thought of my own desperate situation. Would I ever get to Dover?

Yet finally I arrived. When I reached my aunt's beautiful house, with its cheerful windows and tiny garden, I was received by a furious Aunt Betsey.

"Get away from here!" she said to me, shaking her head. "Get going! We don't want little boys here!"

"Please, Aunt," I started to say.

"What?" exclaimed Aunt Betsey.

"Please, Aunt, I am your nephew, David Copperfield . . ."

She was so surprised she had to sit down on the path while I burst into tears.

My Aunt Betsey

In spite of her quirks—such as her obsessive fear of donkeys eating the flowers on her front lawn and her comparisons of my silly deeds to my smarter sister who only existed in her mind—Betsey Trotwood became my benefactor.

She took me into her house, where there also lived poor, childish Mr. Dick, a slightly crazy man determined to write a record of his career. But that task turned out to be very difficult, since he kept filling it with nonsense about King Charles I of England—the king who had been beheaded by his own subjects two centuries earlier. He was obsessed with King Charles's head. Finally Mr. Dick turned his useless manuscript into huge kites that he let sail away. His oddness did not prevent him being, like my aunt, a person of unparalleled goodness.

I owe my good aunt Betsey a good part of my life today. She nicknamed me "Trotter" or "Trot" and sent me to further my education at a school in Canterbury. There I stayed with Aunt Betsey's lawyer, Mr. Wickfield, and his lovely, calm daughter, Agnes, who doted on her widowed father. I finished my studies and went to work at the dusty, cluttered offices of Spenlow and Jorkins as a clerk for Mr. Spenlow.

Dora Spenlow

It was at that time that I met Dora Spenlow, the daughter of my employer, and I fell in love with her at first sight. I was very lonely and ready for romance. I found her beauty and innocence fascinating. We became secretly engaged, and I wrote to her often. Those letters fell into the hands of Miss Murdstone, who was now Dora's paid companion, and who wished to go on causing me harm because she felt an undying hatred for me. One day she came to Mr. Spenlow's office and reported me to my employer. Mr. Spenlow forbid me to continue seeing his daughter and threatened to disinherit her. Those days were very difficult, but my love won out in the end, and I married Dora.

Although Dora was a terrible housekeeper, we were happy together at first. I wished that she was a little less childish and was haunted by the fact that although I knew Dora was devoted to me, she did not understand me. Our characters were too different. I began to realize we weren't suited for one another.

I began writing for a newspaper and magazines. I worked very hard on my book, which, when it was published, was a great success. But I did not let myself be carried away by the praise that was ringing in my ears.

Meanwhile, I hoped that if Dora had a child, she might become more mature. But my wife fell ill, and lost the use of her legs. I would carry her up and down the stairs. Little by little she got worse and had to remain in bed. I missed her company and could not look at her or remember how happy she had been in the past without feeling an immense sadness.

"Don't cry," she told me. "I think I was too young when we married. Is my chair still downstairs?"

"In its usual place," I answered, with tears falling from my eyes.

My wife died shortly afterward.

Agnes Wickfield

But life goes on, and I met Agnes Wickfield again. Agnes's father, Aunt Betsey's lawyer, had fallen into the clutches of Uriah Heep, a sinister rascal full of hatred, greed, and craftiness, who looked like a skeleton and had managed to make himself indispensable to Mr. Wickfield to the point that he dominated him completely. The firm came to be called Wickfield & Heep. It was Mr. Micawber, the friend who had consoled me in the early sorrows of my teenage years in the factory of Murdstone & Grinby, who had ended up being Heep's clerk. It was he who uncovered the villainous schemes of that evil man.

I will never forget the scene in which Uriah Heep saw his evil plots revealed and the enthusiasm with which Micawber exposed all his tricks and falsehood. The cadaverous Uriah was imprisoned for life for defrauding the Bank of England.

From that moment things began to get better, and it seemed that misfortune was taking its leave from my life. Little by little I got to know Agnes, and though the memory of Dora was sweet, I discovered that Agnes had always loved me and I was happier at her side. Where

Dora was silly and impetuous, Agnes was mature and calm. The love I had with Agnes was deeper than the infatuation I had with Dora. She became the light of my life. We married and had three children together.

My task is finished, but I do not wish to finish these pages without mentioning that the good Mr. Micawber was finally able to pay the debts that had always tormented him and lives today in the honorable position of a colonial magistrate in Australia.

My greatest desire is that the face of my dear Agnes should be always close to mine. That when my adventures and misadventures end I can find her at my side with one hand lifted, pointing at the heavens.

1862-1911

Emilio Salgari

Emilio Salgari was an Italian writer who penned over two hundred stories and novels. He wrote swashbuckling adventure tales set in exotic locations, with heroes from various cultures. He was also a pioneer of science fiction in Italy and was sometimes called "the Italian Jules Verne."

His popular novel *Sandokan*, also known as *The Tiger of Malaysia* or *The Tigers of Mompracem*, is part of a cycle of eleven novels about Malayan pirates. These books tell the legend of Sandokan, who was orphaned when British colonialists in Malaysia murdered his family and stole his throne. He turned pirate and swore he would have his vengeance.

Though Salgari's characters achieved fame and he had millions of readers, he never enjoyed the financial success or stability he deserved. His publishers took advantage of his poor business skills, leaving him almost destitute. He committed suicide in 1911. It wasn't until the late twentieth century that Salgari's writings began to receive critical acclaim and new translations started appearing in print.

SANDOKAN

The Pirates of Mompracem

Mompracem was a savage little island in the Sea of Malaysia that was home to a group of terrifying pirates led by the legendary and powerful Sandokan, known as the Tiger of Malaysia. His name wasn't given lightly; he was ferocious and merciless to his enemies. Sandokan's father had been a prince, but Sandokan had been orphaned as a child when his family was murdered by the English and he had been dethroned. Since then he had sworn vengeance on the English and Dutch colonialists.

A violent hurricane lashed Mompracem on the night of December 20, 1849. Thunder and lightning streaked the air in a thousand patterns, tearing through the sky. Heavy rain fell upon the few, mostly fortified buildings. Atop a giant cliff that towered over the sea stood a large hut protected by thick, sturdy walls. Inside the hut was a room carpeted with red silk, cluttered with axes, daggers, European guns, and other weapons, as well as jewels from China and Japan, bars of silver, piles of gold, and vases overflowing with pearls and diamonds.

In that room a young man with a catlike appearance paced restlessly. His dark eyes glowed with a strange fire when he approached the window to contemplate the world outside. He was tall, well built, with a handsome bronzed face and thick black wavy hair that fell freely about his strong shoulders. He had a high forehead, sparkling eyes, and thin lips. A magnificent beard gave his features a proud look that inspired fear and respect. One could tell at first glance that he possessed the ferocity of a tiger and the strength of a giant.

"It's midnight and he has still not returned!" Sandokan said, with a threatening glance at the treasures that surrounded him.

Time passed and the man's impatience grew when the door opened. On the threshold there appeared a figure wrapped in a cloak dripping with rain.

"Yañez! What a horrible night, brother! Come in and drink with me."

"Sandokan!" exclaimed the new arrival in a strong Portuguese accent.

And the two of them sat down at the table.

"Well, Yañez, did you succeed in seeing the girl with the golden hair?" the young man asked his companion, a man of thirty-three or thirty-four years of age. He was tall, with white skin, fine aristocratic features, and light blue eyes. A black mustache curved above his smiling lips. Under the cloak he was dressed with extreme elegance: a brown velvet jacket with gold buttons, brocaded pants, and long boots of red leather. A large sash of blue silk was wrapped about his waist. A scimitar with a hilt of gold, inlaid with a diamond as large as a walnut, hung from his side.

"No," the other answered, "but I can tell you all you want to know."

And he told Sandokan about the lovely girl on the neighboring island of Labuan who had captivated Sandokan's heart before he had even met her. He listened fascinated, until Yañez mentioned the English.

"What are they doing on Labuan, those loathsome Englishmen, who destroyed my family and my lineage?"

"They are building fortifications and preparing to destroy you, just as you destroy their ships."

Sandokan took a few steps across the room, with his arms folded over his chest.

"Good," he said, "we will go to Labuan. Give the order for the lads to prepare themselves, Yañez."

"Don't tempt fate, my brother."

"Silence. Let's go to sleep."

The following morning they embarked with their best men. There were Malays and Battias, Dayaks and Siamese, Indians, Tagalos, and Javanese. All the peoples of those seas were represented in the crews of those two *paraos*, the Philippine ships that were now raising their sails.

"Weigh anchor," Sandokan ordered. And the ships cut across the waves like ill-omened birds, loaded with cannons and pistols.

But the island of Mompracem had disappeared over the horizon. Hours passed and nothing, not a mast, not a sail, gave any indication of the proximity of the pirates' prey. Impatience was beginning to show in the eyes of all when they finally came upon and boarded a Chinese junk, whose resistance was useless, despite the courage of its crew.

The Tiger of Malaysia ordered a new course to Labuan, the island where the blonde girl who so obsessed him lived. Only when dawn was breaking could the silhouette of the island be seen on the horizon.

The Pearl of Labuan

Leaving the pirates on board the *paraos*, Sandokan and one of his men were tramping through the jungle of Labuan. They knew that the lovely woman they were looking for lived very near there, but they were unable to continue their search because a cannon shot coming from the *paraos* caused them to hasten back to the ships. A cruiser belonging to the hated English had discovered them!

They did not run from battle. Steel against wood, oars against steam, they threw themselves into a battle that could only conclude with defeat.

"Kill, kill!" shouted Sandokan to his followers.

He fell, wounded in the chest by a rifle shot, but got up again. Seeing that all was lost, he jumped into the water.

Sandokan would never surrender. He seized a piece of wood that was floating by and drifted for hours, trying to ignore the pain of his wound. At dawn, he again reached the enemy island and looked for refuge in the forest. He found a brook where he could quench his thirst. Then, feeling that he had no strength left, he closed his eyes.

When he came to he realized, to his amazement, that he was in a spacious room, lying on a comfortable bed.

"Where am I?" he wondered.

Suddenly he noticed that at his side was a book. He picked it up and read the name on the cover.

"Marianna!" he said aloud.

It was the first time that he had heard that exotic word and, on repeating it, he felt moved by an unfamiliar emotion, just as the door to his room opened and a European man walked in.

"I am glad to see you are calm now. You have been delirious for three days."

"Three days!" Sandokan exclaimed. "But who are you, sir?"

"Lord James Guillonk, captain in the navy of Her Gracious Majesty, the Empress Victoria of Great Britain."

Sandokan could not help giving a start. He was in the midst of his hated enemies.

"I am," Sandokan said, "the brother of the Sultan of Shaja."

"Then you are a Malayan prince. No doubt you were attacked by pirates and managed to swim to our shores."

"Yes, I held onto a board from one of my ships."

Then they heard someone playing a few chords on a mandolin.

An unexplainable emotion took hold of him, and he could not restrain an exclamation of surprise when a young woman entered the room.

The pirate's heart beat wildly.

"Are you suffering terribly?" asked the girl, explaining that she was Lord Guillonk's niece.

"No longer, my lady, since I am in the presence of the lovely woman known as 'the Pearl of Labuan.'"

When Sandokan was again alone, he felt he could not contain himself. "I'm going mad!" he exclaimed. "I love her!"

The Tiger Hunt

The pirate's recuperation went on for a long time, but the company of Marianna made him forget any longing he might have felt for Mompracem and his concern for the fate of his men. When he had recovered, Lord Guillonk informed him that, along with some friends, he was preparing to set out to hunt a fierce tiger that had been discovered in the region.

"Would you like to accompany us?" he asked. "Lady Marianna will be coming with us as well."

"Naturally I would like to—I burn with desire to find that tiger!"

They went down to the park where more hunters were waiting for them. One of them, an elegant young navy officer, immediately aroused Sandokan's violent dislike. He managed to conceal it, however.

At one point the pirate found himself alone with Marianna in the deepest jungle and, though afraid of being rejected, he confessed to the adoration he felt for her.

"I am certain that you, too, will love me some day, since I am going to make you the queen of the Malaysian seas."

"My goodness! But who are you?" the girl asked.

Sandokan did not answer, and soon the two caught up with the rest of the hunters.

The hunt went on, and Sandokan, armed only with his kris, an elaborate Malay dagger, had to face the wild tiger after it had knocked down the clumsy officer who had missed his shot. Sandokan offered Marianna the skin of the tiger as a gift.

The officer that Sandokan so disliked was beginning to get suspicious. He began to doubt the Malay prince.

"Were you not present at a skirmish between a cruiser and two pirate ships commanded by the Tiger of Malaysia?" he asked at lunch.

"No."

Then the English officer whispered something in Lord Guillonk's ear that no one else could hear. Sandokan knew that he had to leave the mansion that had been his refuge as quickly as possible. But he could scarcely bring himself to separate from his beloved Marianna, who, on her part, warned him of the danger he was in.

"Flee from here! Danger threatens. They are planning something against you!"

And the pirate rushed like a beast through the park, trying to avoid the soldiers who were about to commence the hunt for the fearsome Sandokan.

In his flight the Tiger of Malaysia had the luck to come upon one of his men, another survivor of the battle that had been both his downfall and his good fortune. The two of them, making use of a fragile canoe, set their course for Mompracem. It was only the daring and extraordinary skill of Sandokan that made it possible for them to withstand the fury of the waves and reach the island.

But from the rocky heights the pirate continued to be tormented by love and longing. What might be happening in Labuan? What sorrows might be troubling the lovely Marianna?

The New Crossing

The faithful Yañez was witness to the suffering that Sandokan was overwhelmed by and understood that it was useless to oppose his desires.

They gathered their crews and set out again on the crossing.

"Yañez, I love her! Now I would rather never have been the Tiger of Malaysia, enemy of the English, because my beloved is English."

"Sandokan!" said Yañez, more and more disturbed, "be careful, for we are exposing ourselves to great danger."

Again they crossed the Malaysian Sea, slipping between the English cruisers that patrolled those waters in search of the *paraos* from Mompracem but managed to reach Labuan in spite of all the obstacles.

They landed on the island and easily found the path that led to Lord Guillonk's isolated mansion.

When they reached the park, they approached the Chinese pavilion where Marianna used to go every day to do her embroidery. Yañez lit a match, and on an elegantly carved table they saw a basket with some pieces of cloth inside.

"Are those her things?" Yañez asked.

"Yes," answered the pirate, with infinite tenderness.

Then Yañez took a piece of paper and wrote this note:

We landed. Tonight at midnight we will be under your window.

Provide us with a rope and Sandokan will climb the wall.

Then they retreated to the darkness of the jungle, waiting impatiently for night to come. When night arrived they approached the mansion, but after getting past the guards, they realized that all the windows were barred. It was impossible to get either in or out.

Yañez threw some pebbles at Marianna's window, and she was soon leaning out.

"Sandokan, you've come. But fly, my love, fly. You are in danger!"

The Tiger of Malaysia groaned in desperation. Ought he to leave when he was so close to his beloved? By no means! But Lord Guillonk was already opening the door into Marianna's room, and he pulled her from the window, while the noise of men running and the clatter of their arms warned Sandokan that the soldiers were about to attempt to take him prisoner.

Thus the pirates retreated again, knowing the jungle would protect them, and one day soon Lord Guillonk and Marianna would have to come out of the mansion.

"Then we will attack their escort," said Yañez, "and capture Marianna."

Time passed and one day, disguised in the uniform of an English corporal he had beaten in a fight, Yañez presented himself at the doors of the mansion and asked to be received by Lord Guillonk.

"My lord," he said, "I am a relative of Baronet William, your niece's future husband, and I have come to inform you that we have the Tiger of Malaysia surrounded. The baronet thinks it advisable for you to retire for a few days to Victoria, since he fears that Sandokan with his eighty pirates may attempt to attack the mansion. Would you permit me now to speak to my future relative? I have something to tell her from William."

Once alone with Marianna, Yañez revealed who he was.

"Listen to me, my lady. When you are on your way to Victoria, Sandokan will attack your escort and take you away with him.

"And what of my uncle?"

"Have no fear. We will respect his life."

The Pirate's Queen

Those were days of fear and bloodshed. The English soldiers scoured the jungle in search of Sandokan, but the Tiger of Malaysia was too cunning a prey for his pursuers. Time and again he escaped their clutches and succeeded in getting in contact with the rest of his men, who awaited him on the coast.

Meanwhile, at Lord Guillonk's mansion, the expedition was being prepared which, without their knowing, was to make it possible for Marianna and Sandokan to finally be reunited.

When the lord gave the order the squad began to march, and they had scarcely gone two miles when a soft whistle was heard.

"What is that?" the lord asked, turning to Yañez.

"That means, my lord, that you have been betrayed!"

The battle was short and bloody. Sandokan, holding Marianna in his arms, was able to escape. Weighing anchor with his men, he set his course for Mompracem. The Tiger of Malaysia had finally gained his queen.

1850-1894

Robert Louis Stevenson

Robert Louis Stevenson was a celebrity in his time. A popular Scottish novelist, poet, and essayist, he is most remembered for his novels *Treasure Island*, *Kidnapped*, and *The Strange Case of Dr. Jekyll and Mr. Hyde*, as well as for his children's poetry collection *A Child's Garden of Verses*.

Born in Edinburgh, Scotland, he suffered from ill health in childhood and struggled his whole life against tuberculosis, which made him seek out warm climates. In 1889 he and his family sailed for the South Seas where he ultimately settled on the island of Upolu (now Western Samoa) in the South Pacific Ocean. The people of the island called him *Tusitala* or "teller of tales."

Stevenson started writing at a young age, but his first popular book was *Treasure Island*, published in 1883, a swashbuckling adventure tale about the search for a pirate's buried treasure. Also exceedingly popular was his science-fiction thriller *The Strange Case of Dr. Jekyll and Mr. Hyde*.

TREASURE ISLAND

The Old Pirate Billy Bones

I, Jim Hawkins, write this tale of pirates and gold at the request of others, leaving out nothing but the location of the island where some treasure is still hidden. My mother ran Admiral Benbow's Inn. One day Captain Billy Bones arrived with his trunk. He was a rough-looking man in filthy clothes. He arrived singing an old sea song, "Fifteen men on the dead man's chest—Yo-ho-ho, and a bottle of rum!" He gave me a coin to warn him if I saw any other seamen, especially a sailor with one leg. Every night he sang violent sea songs and drank too much rum. The other guests were both terrified and fascinated by him.

One day a sallow stranger missing two fingers came and asked me for "his mate Bill." I was wary of him and started out to warn the captain, but the stranger prevented me from leaving by holding a cutlass to my throat. When the captain came in and saw the stranger, he looked as startled as if he had seen a ghost or the devil himself.

"Come, Bill, you know me."

"Black Dog," Captain Billy Bones gasped.

"Black Dog as ever was, come for to see his old shipmate Billy."

They sat down at a table to talk, and I served them rum. Soon they were fighting with a great clash of swords. Black Dog ran off wounded, and the captain fell to the floor. We notified Dr. Livesey and he said it was a stroke. When Captain Billy came to his senses he grabbed me by the arm.

"Jim, I'm too weak to run," he said. "Black Dog and others worse than he will return wanting to steal my sea chest. When they come you must call the law on them. They will give me the 'black spot.' I was first mate on the ship of the infamous pirate Captain Flint, and Flint gave me something important before he died."

Before he could tell me what this important thing was, he fell asleep.

The Black Spot

The captain grew weaker and weaker. One day a fearsome blind man came into the tavern. I had never seen such a dreadful-looking figure. He was hunched, tapping a stick as he walked. He wore a green shade over his eyes and nose, as well as a hooded cloak that made him appear deformed. He grabbed my arm in a powerful grip and forced me to take him to Billy. When the old captain saw him, he became terrified. The blind man put a little round piece of paper in the captain's hand and left quickly. The paper was painted black on one side and on the other side were the words: "You have until ten o'clock."

"Six hours. We'll do them yet," the captain said. But as he stood up, he reeled and fell dead on the floor.

I immediately told my mother what had happened. We knew we were in danger, and I reluctantly searched Billy's corpse to find a key to the chest. Inside the chest were papers and some objects of little value. Suddenly we heard the blind man's stick approaching. I grabbed the documents from the trunk, and we ran out of the inn.

Several pirates, under the blind man's direction, broke down the door to the inn. After they realized the captain was dead, they searched the trunk but didn't find what they were looking for.

"Damn my soul! If I had eyes! Look for the boy and his mother!"

At that moment we heard a shot from the hill and some horsemen appeared at a gallop—our salvation! All the pirates disappeared, abandoning the blind pirate who was run down by a man on horseback.

Flint's Treasure

After the authorities rescued us, I decided to take the documents to Dr. Livesey who I found at Squire Trelawney's house. I told them what had happened and gave them the papers.

Trelawney said, "Jim, you have what the pirates were looking for: the map that shows the island where Flint buried his fabled treasure!"

The map showed the position of an island, with its longitude and latitude, and the names of bays and hills. There were three crosses in red ink, two in the north part and one in the south, on which was written, "Bulk of treasure here."

"Livesey," said Squire Trelawney, "I will outfit a ship in the port of Bristol. We will find that treasure."

Long John Silver

Some weeks passed until the ship Hispaniola would be ready to sail. As cook they hired an old sailor called Long John Silver, who helped to gather a crew of the toughest sea dogs. The squire sent me to take a letter to Silver at the Spyglass, a tavern that he ran. He was a very tall, strong man who had lost one leg and carried a crutch under his shoulder, hopping about like a bird. I introduced myself to him.

Silver loudly announced to the crowd that I was their new cabin boy when a customer suddenly left the tavern. I recognized him at once. "It's Black Dog! Stop him!"

"After him!" said Silver. "I don't care who he is, but he owes me money for his drink. That blackguard will never set foot in my house again!"

I told Silver who Black Dog was, and when Silver's men came back empty-handed he apologized for not catching the pirate. On our walk to the ship Silver was a fascinating companion, telling me wild sea stories. He carried a parrot perched on his shoulder that he called Cap'n Flint, because the parrot had once sailed with the notorious pirate. Cap'n Flint was always swearing and calling out, "Pieces of eight! Pieces of eight!"

Voyage

I boarded the *Hispaniola* and met Captain Smollett. He told us he didn't like this voyage or the crew. It was a secret journey that everyone knew about, down to the parrot. Smollett said we didn't know what we were getting ourselves into and that we were running a great risk. But since he had no evidence, Trelawney and Livesey didn't listen to him.

The journey began, and the men worked on deck singing: "Fifteen men on the dead man's chest—Yo-ho-ho and a bottle of rum!" Though it was a calm voyage, and the sailors turned out to be good men, shortly before reaching the island something ominous happened. Just after sunset I had finished my work and was hungry. I ran on deck and had to climb all the way into the apple barrel since there were hardly any apples left.

I was hidden in the barrel when Silver and two of the crew came near and started talking. After listening to them a bit, I understood that I should not come out of the barrel for anything in the world.

"Our plan is to have the squire and the doctor find the treasure with the map they have," said Silver. "Not until the gold is loaded on board do we reveal who we are. We'll kill Smollet, Trelawney, Livesey, and their followers when the time comes."

I was terrified, but in that instant the lookout shouted, "Land ho!" I climbed out of the apple barrel and went to look for my friends. I told them what I had heard: the men of Flint's crew, the fiercest pirates that had ever sailed the seas, were on board the *Hispaniola*, and they all obeyed Silver!

My Onshore Adventures

We dropped anchor. When they saw the island, the men did not obey as they had before. Mutiny was getting closer by the minute. Captain Smollett decided Silver would keep them under control if he were allowed to take the men ashore.

The men were very happy, no doubt thinking they would find the treasure as soon as they struck land. Silver organized their departure but left six men on deck to keep watch on us. Without telling my companions, I decided to sneak ashore with the pirates. I slipped into their boat and when we reached land, I jumped out and fled into the woods as I heard Silver's voice behind me, calling, "Jim! Jim!"

I wandered through the forest until I heard voices. It was Silver and another pirate who was refusing to mutiny. The pirate turned to walk away and I watched as Silver lunged at him and stabbed him to death. Terrified, I ran deeper into the forest.

After stumbling around for a while, a noise caught my attention. I saw something that looked like a monkey or a bear. I took out my pistol and moved toward the shaggy figure, realizing that it was a man. He threw himself to his knees.

"Who are you?" I asked.

"I'm poor Ben Gunn, and I haven't spoken to a soul in three years. Do you happen to have a piece of cheese on you?"

He looked like a beggar, wearing clothes made of goatskin. He told me he was a very rich man. I thought he had gone crazy from being so long in that lonely place, but he insisted.

"I tell you I'm very rich, Jim! Give thanks for having been the first to find me. Tell me, isn't that Flint's ship?"

I told him the story of our voyage. Ben replied that he had been one of Flint's crew. Flint had killed the six men who had helped him bury his treasure, marooning Ben on the island. Ben was now the only living man who knew where Flint's treasure was hidden.

Just then we heard a cannonshot coming from the ship. The fighting had started. The Hispaniola was still anchored in the same place, but now on its mast waved the black pirate flag with its skull and crossbones!

The Stockade

Spying a British flag flying over a stockade, I made a run for it. Ben refused to join me, heading back into the woods and promising to meet up with me later. Inside the stockade I found the squire, the captain, the doctor, and a few loyal men, who had abandoned the ship when the pirates mutinied. They had rowed to shore with arms and provisions.

Early in the morning we saw Silver on the other side of the stockade carrying a white flag of truce. Silver tried to convince Smollett to give him the treasure map, promising that he would take us wherever we wanted on the ship in exchange.

Smollett knew it was a trick. "Tell your men to surrender, and we will take them to England where they will have a fair trial. You will not be able to find the treasure, you do not know how to handle a ship on the ocean—if you don't listen to me, you will all die."

Silver marched off, making threats, and suddenly a group of pirates rushed out of the woods shouting and running toward the stockade, while others fired at us from the woods. Though some of the attackers climbed the protective wall, we knocked them back down. The battle ended, the remaining pirates retreated, and victory was ours—for the moment.

My Sea Adventure

I had my own plans, so while the wounded were being tended to, I silently sneaked out of the stockade. Finding Ben Gunn's little coracle (a kind of canoe), I rowed awkwardly out to the *Hispaniola* where I cut the mooring ropes. Once unanchored, the ship threatened to smash the coracle to pieces, so I was forced to grab hold of the *Hispaniola's* jib, crawl along it, and drop onto the deck. On board I saw a dead pirate and the helmsman, Israel Hands, lying with a knife wound. Hands must have killed the other pirate in a drunken fit. I told Hands that I was in charge now and quickly lowered the pirate flag and threw it overboard. Hands helped me sail the ship to the Northern Inlet. Acting very weak, Hands asked me to cut him some tobacco, and while my back was turned he advanced toward me, knife in hand. I had to climb the mainmast. Hands threw his knife and wounded me in the shoulder. Hurt and surprised, I fired both my pistols at him, and Hands fell dead into the water.

My wound was not serious and I returned to the stockade. I could hear my friends' snoring. I decided to lie down and wait to surprise them with my news as soon as they woke up. As I walked in I accidentally stepped on a sleeping body. A shrill voice sounded in the dark, "Pieces of eight! Pieces of eight!"

It was Cap'n Flint—Silver's parrot! I turned to run, but hands held me. I had been captured by the pirates.

Captain Silver and the Black Spot

"Here's Jim Hawkins!" said Silver. "Shiver my timbers! Dropped in, eh? What a nice surprise for old John!"

"You haven't got the ship anymore," I answered. "I cut the mooring ropes, killed the sailors on board, and took it where no one will ever see it again."

The pirates were ready to murder me, but to my surprise Silver stopped them. Silver and I were left alone as the others went outside to argue. They came back in and huddled together in fear, until one of them came forward timidly. He put something in Silver's hand.

"The black spot! I thought so," Silver said. "You want to depose me. Well, first take a look at this."

And he threw to the floor a yellowish paper with three red crosses. It was the treasure map! The mutineers leaped upon it like cats on a mouse.

"Silver for cap'n!" they all shouted now. Silver had avoided his death and saved my life in the bargain.

It turns out Silver had made a treaty with Dr. Livesey and the others. Why the doctor had given up the map, I couldn't in the least understand. Dr. Livesey came in the morning to attend to the wounded. When he was about to leave, he said that he wished to talk to me. Silver consented in exchange for my promise not to escape, which I agreed to. I told the doctor that the ship was in the North Inlet, run aground in a safe place. The doctor tried to convince me to escape, but I had made a promise. The doctor left with a warning to Silver: "Look out for dangers. I will do what I can for you."

Flint's Ghost

I joined the pirates in their search for the treasure, Silver leading me by a rope. We followed the map and soon found a human skeleton on the ground. Its bony arm pointed in the direction we had to go. The pirates became frightened, fearing Flint's evil spirit.

Suddenly, from out of the trees came a high, trembling voice singing, "Fifteen men on the dead man's chest—Yo-ho-ho and a bottle of rum!"

"It's Flint!" they shouted. I had never seen men more dreadfully affected than those pirates. The color went from the faces, some leaped to their feet, and some clawed hold of others.

"Mates," said Silver through ashen lips, "I've come here to look for gold and nobody, man or devil, will stop me now."

We continued going forward, but when we arrived at the correct spot the pirates were dumbfounded. There was nothing but a big hole in front of us. The treasure had disappeared! Suddenly some shots killed two pirates. Out of the woods came the captain, the doctor, the squire, and Ben Gunn with smoking muskets.

"Ben, Ben," Silver murmured, "and to think it was you that's done me in!"

While we were going down to the boats, we found out that Ben Gunn had discovered the treasure long before and had hid it in a cave. That was why the doctor had given Silver the map; it was no longer good for anything. It was also Ben who had frightened the pirates with the voice of Flint's ghost.

After spending three days carrying the loot from Ben's cave to the ship, we prepared to sail for home. We left the remaining pirates on the island, except for Silver, who joined us until we stopped at a port where he sneaked off, carrying a small portion of the treasure. I never heard of him again.

Back home Squire Trelawney and Doctor Livesey went back to their businesses, Captain Smollet retired from the sea, and Ben Gunn spent all his money within three weeks' time. As for me, I never stopped being haunted by my time on the accursed Treasure Island. The worst dreams I had were when I heard the sharp voice of Captain Flint's parrot ringing in my ears, crying out: "Pieces of eight! Pieces of eight!"

1854-1900

Oscar Wilde

Oscar Wilde (full name Oscar Fingal O'Flahertie Wills Wilde) was an Irish playwright, novelist, poet, and short-story writer. Born in Dublin, Ireland, he later lived in London and Paris. He was one of the most popular dramatists of the late nineteenth century and was famous for his sharp wit and colorful personality.

The Canterville Ghost is a popular 1887 novella, which has been adapted for the stage and screen many times. It pokes fun at the genre of the gothic novel. Gothic stories are tales of terror that often involve ghosts, haunted houses, mysteries, and the supernatural. In addition to *The Canterville Ghost*, Wilde is most celebrated for his novel *The Picture of Dorian Gray* and his play *The Importance of Being Earnest*.

Wilde's life was chaotic. He went from enjoying the fame and admiration of his contemporaries to being put on trial and suffering a dramatic downfall. He was imprisoned for two years in Paris and died penniless at the age of forty-six.

THE CANTERVILLE GHOST

New Owners

When Mr. Hiram B. Otis, the American diplomat, bought Canterville Chase, everyone said that he was a fool because the house was haunted. "We haven't cared to live there," Lord Canterville told him, "since a skeleton rested his hands on my great-aunt's shoulders."

"My Lord," the diplomat answered, "I'll buy the furniture and the ghost, too."

A few weeks later the family arrived at the mansion: Mr. and Mrs. Otis; their eldest son, Washington; their daughter Virginia; and the twins. As soon as the Otises entered the house, the sky went dark.

Mrs. Umney, the housekeeper, served tea in the library. Suddenly Mrs. Otis observed that there was a dull red stain on the floor near the fireplace. "I'm afraid something has been spilled here," she said.

"Yes, madam," the housekeeper replied. "In 1575 Lady Eleanore de Canterville's blood was spilled here, murdered by her own husband, Sir Simon. The tourists admire it very much. The stain cannot be removed."

"How horrid!" exclaimed Mrs. Otis. "I don't care at all for a bloodstain in a sitting room. It must be removed at once. Pinkerton's Champion Stain Remover will clean it up in no time." And kneeling down, she set to work.

"I knew Pinkerton would do it!" she exclaimed triumphantly when no trace of the bloodstain could be seen. At the same instant a terrible clap of thunder resounded outside and Mrs. Umney fainted.

"What nasty weather!" said the ambassador calmly.

"My dear Hiram," cried Mrs. Otis, "what can we do with a woman who faints?"

"Charge her for it," answered the diplomat. As if she had heard, Mrs. Umney came to, muttering, "I have seen things in this house that would make your hair stand on end."

Mr. and Mrs. Otis told her not to be afraid of ghosts, and after getting a raise in her salary the housekeeper tottered off.

The Ghost Appears

The storm raged the whole night, and by the next morning the stain had reappeared.

"I don't think it can be the fault of the detergent," said Washington. "It must be the ghost."

They rubbed out the stain a second time, but the next morning it was there again, and the next day, and the next. Even Mr. Otis began to have his doubts about the nonexistence of ghosts.

That night, after the family went to bed, a curious noise woke Mr. Otis. There was a clanking of metal in the corridor, and it seemed to be drawing nearer. He put on his slippers, opened the door, and in the pale moonlight, he saw an old man with long, gray hair and red eyes like burning coals. His clothes were ragged. Chains hung from his wrists and ankles.

"My dear sir," said Mr. Otis, "I must insist on your oiling those chains. Here is a bottle of Tammany Rising Sun Lubricator. It is very effective. I shall leave it for you and supply you with more, if you require it."

He left the bottle on a marble table and went back to bed.

Indignant, the ghost dashed the bottle violently on the floor and fled down the hallway uttering horrible groans, until he vanished through a wall.

The house remained fairly quiet while the Canterville ghost reviewed his three hundred years of success in terrifying people. He had achieved greatness as a ghost. Never had he been so grossly insulted. He decided he must take revenge.

The Ghost's Vengeance

The next morning the Otis family discussed the ghost. Mr. Otis was a tad offended to find his present had not been accepted.

"I have no wish to do the ghost any personal injury," he said, "but we shall have to take those chains away from him. We can't sleep with that noise."

For the rest of the week the ghost did not disturb them. The bloodstain always reappeared, however. It kept changing color—dull red, yellow, purple—until one morning it had turned emerald green.

The second appearance of the ghost took place on Sunday night, shortly after the Otis family had gone to bed. They heard a terrific crash, and downstairs they found a suit of armor on the floor and the Canterville ghost seated on a chair, rubbing his knees in agony. The twins used him as a target for their peashooters, and Mr. Otis pointed his revolver at him, which obliged the ghost to make his escape. When he had reached the top of the stairs, though, and was somewhat recovered, he offered his audience an example of his most diabolical laughter.

The fearful echo had hardly died away when Mrs. Otis came out saying, "I am afraid you are far from well. I have brought you a bottle of Doctor Dobell's medicine. It is an excellent remedy for indigestion."

Dejected, the ghost broke down when he reached his room. The twins were absolutely vulgar and Mrs. Otis was materialistic. But what distressed him most was that he had been unable to wear the suit of mail. He had hoped that even modern Americans would be spooked by the sight of a specter in armor!

Feeling ill, the ghost scarcely left his room for several days, except to replace the bloodstain. He then decided to make a third attempt to frighten the Otis family. As he walked down the hallway thinking over his elaborate plan he chuckled to himself. Then suddenly he wailed in terror. He had bumped into a horrible specter with scarlet eyes and a mouth full of fire. Never having seen a ghost before, he was naturally frightened and fled back to his room. After a time, the Canterville ghost decided he must speak to the other ghost. He returned to the grisly phantom and finally understood the Otises' trick.

The ghost turned out to be a white curtain, a kitchen cleaver, a hollow turnip, and a sign that read:

THE OTIS GHOST.
THE ONLY TRUE SPOOK.
BEWARE OF IMITATIONS.

He had been outwitted! His nerves were completely shattered. He decided to give up the business of the bloodstain in the library. If the Otis family did not want it, clearly they did not deserve it. His other obligations as a ghost were another matter. His solemn duty was to appear in the hallway once a week and to mutter from the bay window on the first and third Wednesdays of the month. But he took precautions to avoid making unnecessary noises—he wore slippers—and even came to use, to his shame, the Tammany Rising Sun Lubricator to oil his chains. In spite of everything, however, he was still abused. Strings were stretched across the hallway, and he tripped over them in the dark. The last insult was when he fell on his face after slipping on the butter the twins had smeared on the floor.

He now gave up all hope of ever frightening this rude American family.

The Prophecy

One day, young Virginia went riding with her suitor, the Duke of Cheshire, and she tore her dress on some brambles. She returned home and, coming up the back stairs, she thought she saw someone in the tapestry room. She found the Canterville ghost looking discouraged. His expression was so forlorn that Virginia took pity.

"I'm sorry for you," she said, "but my brothers are going off to boarding school tomorrow and if you behave yourself no one will annoy you."

"It is absurd asking me to behave myself. I must rattle my chains and frighten people. It is my only reason for existing."

"That is not a reason for existing. You have been very wicked. You stole my paints to restore that ridiculous bloodstain. First you took all my reds, then my yellow, and my emerald green—whoever heard of emerald green blood?"

"What was I to do?" The ghost asked meekly. "It is very difficult to get real blood nowadays."

"Mrs. Umney told us how evil you were. It is very bad to go about killing people—especially your own wife."

"I admit that was bad, but it was a family matter and concerned no one else."

But they went on talking, and the ghost felt himself being won over by Virginia's honesty and sweetness.

"Please don't go," he begged her. "I am so lonely. I want to go to sleep and I can't. I haven't slept for three hundred years."

"Poor ghost," Virginia murmured. "Have you no place where you can sleep?"

"Have you ever read the old prophecy on the library window?"

"Of course!" Virginia recited, "'When a golden girl can win prayer from out the lips of sin, when the barren almond bears, and a little child gives away its tears, then shall all the house be still and peace come to Canterville.' But I don't know what it means."

"It means that you must cry for my sins, because I have no tears. And pray for my soul to the Angel of Death, because I have no faith."

"I'm not afraid. I'll ask the angel to take pity on you," Virginia said to him.

The ghost got up with a cry of joy and, pulling her along with frozen fingers, he led her across the dark room.

"Quickly," he cried, "or it will be too late."

The Ghost Is Freed

When Virginia did not come down to tea, Mr. Otis sent someone to look for her. But his daughter was nowhere to be found. The young Duke of Cheshire was frantic and accompanied Mr. Otis to the police, but no one could give them any information. They returned home, finding young Washington and the twins looking very sad. Mrs. Otis, who was beside herself, was having her forehead bathed with eau-de-cologne.

The diplomat then ordered a cold supper to be served. They were about to leave the dining room when they heard loud thunder, strange music, and a panel at the top of the staircase flew open.

Suddenly, there was a very pale Virginia.

"My God! Where have you been?" Mr. Otis said.

"Papa, I've been with the ghost. He's dead. He has been very wicked, but he was sorry for all he had done. He gave me this box of jewels before he died."

"What an angel you are!" cried the young Duke, kissing her.

"Look," one of the twins exclaimed, pointing to the window, "the withered almond tree has blossomed."

"God has forgiven him!" Virginia whispered gravely.

Four days later a funeral coach left Canterville Chase pulled by eight black horses. Lord Canterville had arrived to attend his ancestor's funeral, and Virginia sat by his side in the carriage. When the coffin was lowered into the grave, a nightingale sang.

Mr. Otis wanted to give Lord Canterville his ancestor's jewels back. "My dear sir," answered the lord, "your daughter has done my unfortunate ancestor a service that is far more valuable."

Virginia, years later, wore those jewels at her wedding to the Duke of Cheshire.

"You have never told me what happened when you were locked up with the ghost, Virginia," her husband said to her one day.

"Please don't ask me, Cecil. I cannot tell you. The ghost made me see that love is stronger than Life and Death."

"You can keep your secret as long as I have your heart. But you will tell our children some day, won't you?"

And Virginia blushed.

1802-1870

Alexandre Dumas

Alexandre Dumas (born Dumas Davy de la Pailleterie) was a renowned French
novelist of swashbuckling adventure stories whose masterpieces include *The Three
Musketeers* and *The Count of Monte Cristo*. He wrote many other popular novels
such as *The Man in the Iron Mask*, *Twenty Years After*, and *The Black Tulip*.

Though best known as a novelist, Dumas first earned his success as a dramatist.
He also wrote numerous articles. Dumas made extensive use of ghostwriters,
Auguste Maquet being the best known. Maquet outlined the plot of *The Count of
Monte Cristo* and contributed greatly to *The Three Musketeers* and its sequels.

Dumas was a huge celebrity author in his day, almost as famous for his lavish
lifestyle and reckless spending as for his masterful writing. In fact, Dumas was often
in debt. Along with Mark Twain and Robert Louis Stevenson, Dumas remains an
acclaimed nineteenth century writer who has retained his popularity.

THE COUNT OF MONTE CRISTO

Château d'If

It was February 24, 1815. At the port of Marseilles, the watchtower gave the signal that the ship *Pharaon* was in sight. Soon it passed Château d'If, an isolated island prison, and came into port. Morrel, the ship's owner, went aboard immediately and noticed the sailors were unusually sad. He went up to Edmond Dantès, a handsome, dark-eyed lad of about twenty.

"What has happened, Edmond? What's the meaning of these long faces I see on the crew?"

"A great misfortune. Our captain, Leclerc, has died."

"Did he fall into the sea?"

"No, sir. He died of brain fever. Here comes Mr. Danglars, our purser, who will inform you of the details." Edmond left to help drop the ship's anchor and dock the ship at the port.

Danglars said, "Well, Mr. Morrel, you know of our misfortune. What made things worse was that as soon as the captain died, Edmond took over the ship and made us waste a day and a half at the island of Elba."

This surprised Morrel very much. Elba was where the deposed emperor Napoléon was being held prisoner. And it was illegal for any French subject to communicate with him. Danglars was very suspicious that Edmond had not only met with Napoléon personally, but he agreed to deliver a note to Paris for him.

Truly, though, Danglars held a more personal grudge against Edmond that he did not mention to Morrel. He resented how Captain Leclerc passed him over to promote Edmond instead of himself.

When Morrel asked Edmond for an explanation, he reassured him that he made the visit and the promise only as a favor to Captain Leclerc, a good man. Edmond felt the debt he owed to his captain and friend was more important than others' disapproval of the former emperor. Morrel agreed that it was an honorable thing to do and allowed Edmond to leave the ship.

Edmond was so happy to be home in Marseilles. As soon as the ship had anchored, Edmond ran to his father's house. With great emotion he embraced the old man, whose tears were a sign of the pride he felt in his son. Then Edmond hurried to see his fiancée, Mercédès, the loveliest girl in Marseilles, who was waiting for him. He hoped to marry her right away.

"Mercédès ! Mercédès !" he cried, while the girl, blushing with happiness and love, threw herself into his arms. But this affection infuriated another man, Fernand, who was also in the room.

"Ah," said Edmond, frowning, "I hadn't realized there were three of us."

"It doesn't matter, Edmond," said Mercédès. "From now on he will be your best friend because he is my cousin Fernand, the man I love most next to you."

But when Edmond cordially offered his hand, Fernand did not move, showing the jealousy he felt.

After Fernand left the lovers, he secretly met up with Danglars in a tavern. Together they drank to their mutual hatred for Edmond. Remembering Edmond's visit to Elba and knowing that he was also about to go to Paris, they concluded that he must be spying for Napoleon.

"That gives me an idea," Danglars murmured.

The Arrest of Edmond Dantès

The day of Edmond and Mercédès's wedding dawned magnificently, but before the couple had pronounced their vows, when they were still at the banquet, the door opened and in walked a police inspector, four soldiers, and a corporal who, with no hesitation at all, took poor Edmond prisoner.

The fathers of both Mercédès and Edmond were terribly upset, but powerless to stop the arrest. No one knew what the young man was accused of doing. Some said it was for smuggling goods on the Pharaon. But the true reason for his arrest was that Danglars and Fernand had informed the king's deputy in Marseilles, Villefort, that Edmond was conspiring with the banished emperor Napoleon to overthrow the French government. Both men were willing to abuse justice for their own selfish desires.

Morrel, the shipowner, begged Villefort to release Edmond. Villefort agreed to give the prisoner a chance to defend himself.

"Did you serve under the tyrant, Napoleon?" he asked. "They say you have dangerous political ideas."

"Political ideas, sir?" replied Edmond. "I am almost ashamed to say I have never had any."

And, trusting the deputy, Edmond explained that his visit to Elba and carrying of the letter was only out of loyalty to his dead captain. He realized this letter must now be in Villefort's possession, since he could see the objects that had been taken from him on his arrest laid out on the deputy's table.

"Have you read this letter?" Villefort asked.

"Oh no!"

"Do not speak to anyone about it. That would be the end of you." Villefort took out a match. "You see how I am burning it now. The main charge against you now no longer exists, and you will be freed very soon."

But he was lying to Edmond. Ringing the bell, Villefort summoned the police inspector and said a few words in his ear.

Poor Edmond Dantès did not know that his fate had just been sealed. Villefort had realized, on reading the letter, that his own father had been implicated in a Napoléonic plot. With the secret instructions to the inspector, he hoped to avoid any damage to his reputation. And so, Villefort became the third man to do wrong to Edmond for his own personal gain.

Edmond was immediately taken to Château d'If, the most terrible dungeon in the kingdom of France, where unhappy prisoners rotted slowly, completely isolated from the rest of the world.

Many years passed. Edmond had lost all hope. The only human contact he had was with his jailers, until another prisoner, the Abbot Faria, dug a tunnel between their two cells. The abbot was hoping to escape through the tunnel, but was too old and weak to continue digging by himself. Edmond helped him, hoping that together they both could escape one day. Meanwhile, they became close friends through their long secret talks. Edmond learned much from the wise old man. The abbot taught him about philosophy, languages, and mathematics. When Abbot Faria fell ill for the final time and was approaching death, he told Edmond of his greatest secret: a great treasure belonging to a Cardinal Spada, a treasure whose existence and location was known only to him. He once even tried to bribe his jailers with promise of this treasure, but the guards had always simply called him a madman.

When Abbot Faria died, Edmond heard the jailers pack away his body in a sack and thought of a brilliant escape plan. When the jailers left the abbot's cell, he rushed down the tunnel the abbot had dug and took the dead man's place in the sack.

He kept in his hand a small piece of metal that he had been using as a digging tool to rip open the sack once it was buried.

Edmond was relieved when the guards did not notice that the bodies had been switched. But he became frightened when instead of burying him as he expected, they threw the sack into the sea! Even worse, they had attached a cannonball to make sure it sank down to the very bottom.

But Edmond remained brave. As soon as he hit the water, he cut himself out of the sack and, after fourteen years of wrongful imprisonment, Edmond Dantes regained his freedom and swam to shore.

Strange Events

The following day Edmond discovered that his appearance had changed so much no one could recognize him. It was necessary to begin a new life. Using his knowledge of navigation, he joined a ship of smugglers that would pass close to the island of Monte Cristo, where the Abbot Faria told him the treasure of Cardinal Spada could be found.

These were days of great intensity. The sea air enhanced his new sensation of freedom, as well as his hatred for those who had done him so much injustice.

When the Island of Monte Cristo finally came into view, Edmond persuaded the captain of the little ship to drop him off on the jagged coast and promise to return to pick him up. The captain obliged.

Soon Edmond found himself alone on the shores of Monte Cristo. Discovering that the place corresponded exactly to what Abbot Faria had described, he exclaimed, "Open Sesame!"

While thousands of cicadas made their monotonous chirping sound, he crossed the island on foot under a burning sun. He felt a strange emotion as he approached the caves that, according to the abbot, hid the great treasure. His heart beat wildly, and he could hardly control his desire to shout. With an effort he pushed aside an enormous rock that covered the passageway and watched it roll down the steep hillside and plunge into the sea. Entering a circular opening, he noticed an iron ring at the center of a great square slab. The rest was only a question of strength, and at last he opened up the great chest full of immense wealth.

When, as agreed, the smuggling ship came back for him, Edmond had already carefully hidden the treasure, but not before filling his pockets with jewels and gold coins that would enable him to carry out the plan he had in mind.

A Mysterious Stranger

A short time later a stranger arrived in Marseilles who bestowed blessings on anyone who had helped Edmond Dantès in any way. He also made inquiries about what had happened to Edmond's father and to Mercédès, the lovely girl Edmond was going to marry that unlucky morning. The stranger also asked for information on the men who had plotted Edmond's misfortunes.

The mysterious stranger learned that Edmond's father had died of sorrow. On his deathbed he had received the comforts only of Mercédès and the shipowner Morrel. He also learned that Mercédès, after having waited for him desperately for eighteen months, had ended up marrying her cousin Fernand, who had returned to his native Spain, offered his services to the king, and obtained the honors and wealth that he now enjoyed in France. The stranger learned that the evil Villefort went on to a brilliant career and was married with two sons. Danglars had amassed a great fortune as a banker.

Meanwhile, Morrel was in deep financial trouble and had been forced to go into debt with a powerful English bank. His fate depended on the arrival of his ship, the *Pharaon*, loaded with exotic merchandise, but, according to rumors, it had sunk to the bottom of the sea.

But Morrel soon received a strange visit from a pleasant English banker who offered to extend his debts by three months. Then, just as this period was about to end, to the joy and surprise of all the world, the Pharaon made its triumphal entry into the port of Marseilles. What Morrel did not know was that this was really an exact replica of his ship, built with money from the treasure of Cardinal Spada.

Yes, the stranger was none other than Edmond Dantès, in a variety of disguises. The ease with which he now blended into elite society was in no small part due to the wisdom he learned from the old Abbot Faria during their years as prisoners in the Château d'If.

But only the first part of Edmond's work had now ended. Those who had helped him and shown him friendship found themselves rewarded. Now he decided that the hatred he felt for his enemies must begin.

"Good-bye to human kindness!" he said to himself.

Revenge and Redemption

Soon another stranger appeared in France. An unusual count established himself in Paris and made an immediate impression on the high society of that capital with his generosity, wealth, and elegance. When he claimed to be The Count of Monte Cristo, no one could imagine how such wealth could have come from such a barren island. But, then again, no one knew that this "count" was so skilled in the use of disguises that one moment he would appear dressed as a friar and the next with the stiff demeanor of an English banker!

The three evildoers who years before had brought about the fall of young Edmond Dantes were now enjoying lives of luxury in Paris. Fernand had received the title of Count of Morcerf. He had a son with Edmond's beloved Mercédès, named Albert. Returning from a trip to Rome, Albert was miraculously saved from some fierce Italian bandits by none other than the Count of Monte Cristo. When he told his parents of this adventure, the count was invited to the Morcerfs' home, where Edmond finally saw, after many, many years, the lovely Mercédès, his lost fiancée. Many years had gone by, but to him she was more beautiful than ever. But although she welcomed him very warmly for saving her son, he could not yet reveal to her his true identity.

Meanwhile Edmond, thanks to his immense fortune, was able to bankrupt, little by little, the infamous Danglars, now one of the most wealthy bankers in Europe. Edmond would never forget how the former purser of the Pharaon had sold him out to Villefort under the false accusation of treason, all for the sake of Captain Leclerc preferring Edmond to him.

Neither did Villefort escape Edmond's curse for years of imprisonment needlessly suffered in the dungeons of the Château d'If. By coincidence, Edmond's old friend Morrel, the shipowner, now had a son named Max who was in love with Villefort's daughter Valentine. While protecting Valentine from harm, the Count of Monte Cristo still helped inspire her conniving stepmother to plot against Villefort for the family inheritance. Villefort saw one disaster after another befall his loved ones and finally went mad from the violence he saw unleashed in his own family, including a plot by his second wife to poison Valentine.

Edmond's revenge against Fernand was the most complicated of all his plots, since it involved possibly hurting the person he loved the most, Mercédès. First the count exposed all the private and political scandals that gave Fernand his title and power.

But Fernand's son, Albert, resented the count so strongly for the damage to his father's reputation, that even though he owed Edmond his life, he challenged him to a duel.

The Count of Monte Cristo never refused a duel, and his skill with arms was well known. Mercédès, fearing for the life of her son, went in search of the count to beg him to call it off. But it was then that she finally saw who he really was: her beloved Edmond, whom she had believed dead for over twenty years. The Count of Monte Cristo became Edmond Dantès once again and let his heart be moved. When Albert discovered that his father was in fact a villain after all, he apologized to the count. Fernand eventually killed himself in disgrace, after which Mercédès and Albert left the country to be free of their tortured past. Mercédès and Edmond never saw each other again.

The moral conflicts presented by his plots against Villefort and Fernand caused Edmond to question the justness of revenge. He worried he was punishing more people than just his enemies. And so the count returned to the peace and tranquility of his island of Monte Cristo, accompanied by young Max Morrel and his fiancée, Valentine Villefort. One morning while Max and Valentine were walking alone along the coast, a sailor brought them a surprise note saying:

Live then and be happy with the rest of my treasure, good friends. And never forget that all human wisdom is to be summarized in two words: TRUST AND WAIT!

Your friend,
Edmond Dantès, Count of Monte Cristo

"Who knows if some day we will see him again!" said young Morrel, drying a tear as he saw a sail disappearing over the horizon. "Darling," Valentine replied, "you know what he has told us—trust and wait!"

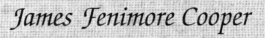

1789-1851

James Fenimore Cooper

James Fenimore Cooper was a prolific and popular American writer of the
early nineteenth century, particularly famous for his novel *The Last of the
Mohicans*, which is considered a literary masterpiece. He's also noted for
the historical romances featuring Nathaniel "Natty" Bumppo, a frontiersman,
in the *Leatherstocking Tales*. Among his other noted titles are
The Pathfinder, *The Deerslayer*, and *The Prairie*.

Born in Burlington, New Jersey, Cooper received an excellent classical
education. As a young man, he sailed in the merchant marine and as
a midshipman in the United States Navy.

Cooper wrote thirty-four novels, some involving sea adventures and others
about the intersection of European and Native-American cultures. While
praised by many contemporaries as "the American Scott," (referring to the
beloved Scottish writer Sir Walter Scott), Mark Twain harshly criticized
Cooper in his satirical essay "Fenimore Cooper's Literary Offences."

THE LAST OF THE MOHICANS

The Trail

In 1757 the English colonies of North America were at war with the French, who recruited Native-American tribes as allies to help fight in the deep forests, swiftly flowing rivers, and dangerous mountains of the New World. This became known as the French and Indian War.

At Fort William Henry, in the wilderness of western New York State, English soldiers were cut off from the rest of their army and surrounded by French troops. The commander of the fort, Colonel Munro, wanted his two daughters, Alice and Cora, brought to him from nearby Fort Edward. Orders were given to a young English officer, Duncan Heyward, to escort the girls on the dangerous journey through enemy territory.

When they set out on horseback, guarded by a group of six English soldiers, an Indian scout, Magua, joined them, causing one of the girls to shriek, thinking he was an enemy.

"Don't be afraid, Alice," Duncan told her. "He's a friend who will be guiding us along this strange, unfamiliar trail."

"I don't like that man," Alice replied.

"Yes, I know. Magua is a Huron, an Indian tribe that is friendly with the French, but he is now on our side."

Two hours later, the young women felt tired and asked to stop along the trail. Duncan ordered Magua to halt the march.

"Not here," Magua said, "farther on there is a clearing where we can rest."

But within moments the party was attacked by a volley of musket shots from the woods. It was a group of Hurons, Magua's tribe, who were fighting for the French.

Duncan tried to protect the girls, when a tall, muscular man, dressed as a hunter, appeared with another tribe, attacking the Hurons from behind. Even though they were saved, the colonel's daughters seemed scared of these fierce warriors.

"You have nothing to fear," the hunter told them. "They're Mohicans. The last of their tribe."

Duncan asked these men to travel with them to the fort. The hunter accepted, but first swore them all to secrecy about the hidden path they would be taking.

They crossed the river and entered a cave secluded behind a waterfall. "Here we will be safe," the hunter said. "This is our refuge."

There the travelers were able to rest and get back their strength. Cora admired the fine features of Uncas, the young Mohican who had led the attack on the Hurons. His strong, determined expression was calming and reassuring.

"The Hurons have not taken us prisoner yet and we can prevent them from entering," Duncan said.

"With what?" the hunter asked. "With arrows? With the ladies' screams?"

Alice interrupted, "The Indians only want us in order to force my father to do what they want. They won't kill us. Save yourselves and go get reinforcements to free us."

"Perhaps you're right," the hunter admitted. And they went off in search of help.

Duncan took the girls to the back of the cave. But they had forgotten about Magua, the Huron guide who pretended to be their friend but actually betrayed them to his tribe. When Magua found them in the cave, he gave a long shout of joy.

All were taken prisoner. The Hurons put the girls on two horses, but they made Duncan walk the road on foot, with his hands tied behind his back. Duncan hoped the march would be long, so that their Mohican friends would have time to find help.

They traveled through the forest for hours and hours, and the prisoners were so overcome by weariness that when the group stopped for the night they fell asleep at once.

When Duncan opened his eyes, the Hurons were arguing loudly. One suddenly took out his knife and, with a menacing look on his face, rushed toward Duncan, knocked him down, and pressed his knees against his chest. Duncan saw the glint of the knife and just when he thought he was done for, a rifle shot rang out. The weight that was crushing his chest was lifted, and his attacker fell dead at his side.

It was the hunter who had come to the rescue. And Uncas, the young Mohican, shouted his war cry as he swiftly attacked. More shots quickly ended the lives of another three Hurons. Some Hurons hid behind Duncan and the girls to use them as shields, but the Mohicans were smart enough not to shoot their friends. Magua, the Huron traitor, seized Cora by her braids and threw her to the ground, but Uncas leaped upon the enemy. Frightened of fighting Uncas, Magua rolled down the steep hillside and plunged into the woods to escape. Cora was very grateful to Uncas for saving her life.

At the Fort

The travelers were now able to pass unharmed through the rest of their journey. They were guided by the hunter, who they now learned was called Hawkeye. And thanks to Duncan's knowledge of French, they were able to trick two guards of the French army.

When one day a thick fog came up, the conditions seemed right to break through the French lines and reach the fort, where Colonel Munro was eagerly awaiting his daughters. They climbed the hills and went down the other side of the mountain.

However, when they tried to cross, they heard a voice.

"Who goes there?" it shouted. They were silent. Then a hail of bullets almost took the lives of the girls and their rescuers, until Alice realized something. The bullets were coming from the soldiers in the fort.

"Father, father!" shouted Alice. "It's us, your daughters!"

The shooting stopped immediately and the gates were opened to receive them. Colonel Munro was greatly relieved to see his daughters alive and safe at last.

Having completed their mission, Hawkeye and the Mohicans took their leave that very night, taking advantage of a break in the French attack.

Since the fort was surrounded by the French and Colonel Munro did not have enough troops to attack them, the girls and Duncan's men had to endure weeks of hardship and deprivation. No reinforcements arrived, and it seemed as though they had been forgotten by the English army.

During the fifteen days of this siege, Duncan had fallen in love with Alice. He decided he must speak to Colonel Munro.

"Sir, I would like to speak with you."

"I was just about to send for you," answered the colonel urgently.

"I want you to know that I would like to marry your daughter Alice."

"Duncan, you wish to be my son and that is an honor for me."

Then the colonel suddenly frowned. "But I want to talk to you about something else. The messenger I sent to get help has not returned,and I am afraid he has fallen into the hands of the French. I am going to ask for a

truce with the enemy. We
will meet between the fort and their
camp. Because you speak French so well, I
want you to be the interpreter."

Duncan knew this would mean surrender but agreed to
help. His job would be to translate between the colonel and
the commander of the French, General Montcalm.

The Massacre

With Duncan's help, Colonel Munro and General Montcalm agreed that
in exchange for abandoning the fort, the English would be treated with
the respect due to their status as soldiers. They could keep their guns
and their flags after surrendering in this most honorable fashion.

But in spite of the promises of the French, the Hurons had no
intention of obeying the agreement. When the English marched out of
the fort they launched a surprise ambush, led by the wicked Magua. The
English soldiers took their positions to repel the attack, but they had little
gunpowder and soon fell into the hands of the Hurons.

Magua had held a grudge against Munro for many years and now took it
out on his daughters. When he found Cora in hiding, he startled her.

"What a pleasant surprise to meet again!"

"Get away!" shouted Cora, covering her eyes in order not to see him.

"Magua is a great chief and your father treats him like a servant.
Magua's revenge will be to take his daughters from him."

He stooped over, grabbed Cora in his arms, and rushed away with her toward the woods. "Stop, stop!" Cora shouted again and again.

The other Hurons found and captured Alice. But Magua wanted Cora all to himself.

The Chase

To rescue the girls, Duncan and Colonel Munro joined with Hawkeye and two of the Mohicans, the brave Uncas and his honorable father, Chingachgook. With Uncas leading the way, the five men moved slowly and cautiously. Uncas and Chingachgook scanned the woods with skilled eyes that could detect the smallest sign of danger. Even though they themselves had miraculously escaped, Duncan and the colonel felt the terrible sorrow of losing Alice and Cora in the massacre.

Their feet trudged forward wearily. Suddenly Uncas gave a start when he found a piece of Cora's shawl on a branch.

"Uncas will try to find her," the young Mohican said as he took the cloth in his hand. "They are leaving a trail for us." He remembered the beautiful Cora and wanted to prove his love for her.

Meanwhile, Duncan noticed on the ground a necklace that Alice had been wearing that very morning. His love for Alice stirred him to action. "Let us not lose an instant," he said.

But Hawkeye advised calm. "The deer that runs the most is not the one that makes for the longest hunt," he said. "Our expedition will take days and nights and an Indian never begins this sort of adventure without taking some time to rest and think."

So they began the search early the next morning. For three days, the men moved forward, careful not to miss any sign of the prisoners.

On the morning of the fourth day, Hawkeye seemed more alert than ever and never ceased glancing about him. Uncas had a look of triumph on his face.

"We've arrived!" the hunter exclaimed. "The Hurons are here!"

Duncan went in search of the girls. But just as he approached the camp and could see them, he was discovered by Magua.

Duncan spat at Magua. "I despise you and your vengeance," he said.

"Will you speak the same way when you are tied to the torture stake?" asked Magua with a cynical smile.

Meanwhile, Hawkeye had disguised himself with a bearskin to enter the camp unnoticed. He freed Alice and Cora and took them to where the colonel and the two Mohicans were waiting. But there was no time to rejoice. They had to get away immediately, before their trick was discovered.

They found refuge in the tents of the Delaware Indians, famous for their hospitality. But Magua and his Hurons soon followed their trail and ordered the Delawares to give Cora back to them, because, they claimed, she belonged to Magua. The Delawares, out of respect for Magua's authority, agreed.

Uncas made plans to rescue his beloved Cora and, with Duncan and the colonel, prepared an attack.

The struggle was long and difficult, full of tricks and skirmishes. Uncas charged furiously upon the Hurons, while Duncan and Hawkeye fired their muskets again and again.

Uncas finally caught up with Magua, who had dragged Cora off with him. He jumped from a cliff onto Magua's back, and the two warriors fought each fiercely, hand-to-hand. When Uncas finally broke free to rescue Cora, he saw that she was already dead. The Hurons had killed her. Uncas swore revenge against the tribe, but before he could fight back, Magua stabbed him in the back. It was to be the last of Magua's many evil deeds because Hawkeye, lifting his musket to his shoulder, put an end to him.

But of course Hawkeye was too late to save either the beautiful Cora or the noble young Uncas. The next morning he and Chingachgook buried the fallen lovers together.

"Brother, you are not alone," Hawkeye told Chingachgook at his son's grave. "Here lies the last of the Mohicans. But though our color is different, our path is the same."

1835-1910

Mark Twain

Born in a small Missouri town as Samuel Langhorne Clemens, this American writer, humorist, and lecturer is better known by his pen name Mark Twain (his pseudonym comes from a Mississippi riverboat term). He is most famous for his two classic novels based on his childhood, *The Adventures of Huckleberry Finn* and *The Adventures of Tom Sawyer*, both of which remain widely taught in school literature classes.

As a young man, Twain worked as a printer's apprentice, a Mississippi riverboat pilot, and a newspaper reporter. He turned from journalism to travel writing and then to fiction. Some of his other noted fictional works are *A Connecticut Yankee in King Arthur's Court*, *The Prince and the Pauper*, and the short story, "The Celebrated Jumping Frog of Calaveras County."

Twain enjoyed great popularity, earning a reputation for wit, and toured widely as a celebrated public speaker. The American author William Faulkner called him "the father of American literature." Twain traveled extensively and his writing was recognized all over the world for its humor, charm, and evocative depiction of a lost America.

THE ADVENTURES OF TOM SAWYER

"Tom!" the old lady shouted, "Tom!"

Silence.

"Where's that scoundrel hiding now?"

Aunt Polly readjusted her glasses and punched the broom under the bed, but only a cat rushed out. Then she heard a noise behind her and grabbed a small boy by his jacket.

"Look at your hands, Tom! Look at your face! I've told you a thousand times not to touch the jam. Give me the switch! Saturday, you're punished. You have to whitewash the fence."

Tom was not the model boy of the village. He knew the model boy very well—and hated him. He often got a whipping from Aunt Polly, his dead mother's sister, but she never hit very hard, because the old lady was softhearted.

When Saturday morning came, the world was bright and brimming with life. Tom reluctantly picked up the bucket of whitewash and the big brush. He surveyed the fence and all gladness left him. He wanted to swim in the Mississippi River with his friends. Soon the other boys would come along and make fun of him for having to work –the thought burned him like fire. But at this dark and hopeless moment an inspiration burst upon him!

"Ha, ha, ha! You're getting it, ain't you?" his friend Ben Rogers called out.

Tom kept painting. He didn't answer.

"I'm going swimming. You coming with me?"

"No," Tom answered. "I like painting too much."

And stepping back to see what his work looked like, he seemed quite pleased with what he was doing. His friend found that very interesting.

"Say, Tom, let me whitewash a little," he said.

"Ben, I'd like to, but not on your life. Aunt Polly is very particular, and you have to do it really carefully."

"Oh, shucks, I'll be careful. And I'll give you a piece of my apple."

Tom gave him the brush, acting reluctant, and then sat down in the shade of his favorite tree looking like a retired artist. When Ben got weary, more of Tom's friends came by, clamoring to do the whitewashing.

When Aunt Polly saw the job finished, she was surprised and pleased.

"Well, I never! Go and play. But if you're late, I'll tan you!"

Tom skipped out and headed into town. As he was passing the house his friend Jeff Thatcher lived in, he saw a lovely blond girl he had never seen before. His heart gave a leap and a certain Amy Lawrence, who he had loved to distraction for some months, immediately vanished out of his heart like a stranger whose visit is done.

He tried to get this new angel's attention, and when he saw he had succeeded, he pretended he didn't know she was there and began to show off to win her admiration.

The girl did not show much interest in his silly gymnastics, but before she went into the house she tossed a flower over the fence. Tom stood outside her window until a maid came and dumped a pitcher of water on his head.

On Sunday morning, Tom didn't want to wash or read the Bible, but he was forced to do both. Later he sat next to Aunt Polly in church. Bored, he took his prized beetle (his "pinchbug") out from a pillbox, but it bit his finger. The beetle fell on the floor as a poodle wandered down the church aisle. The poodle sat down on the beetle and received a big pinch. The dog started yelping and laughter interrupted the sermon. Tom was cheered up.

On Monday Tom walked to school. He met Huckleberry Finn, the son of the town drunk, and the boy that was most dreaded by all the mothers of the town for being lazy, vulgar, and disobedient. Tom, like all the other respectable boys, admired him greatly and played with him every chance he got.

"Hello, Huckleberry!" Tom greeted the outcast.

"Hello, yourself! Look, a dead cat. I bought him off a boy. Cats are good for curing warts."

"I know something better," said Tom. "Spunk water. You go to the woods at midnight, stick your hand in a tree trunk that's got rainwater in it, say, 'Barleycorn, barleycorn, injun-meal shorts. Spunk water, spunk water, swaller these warts,' and turn around three times."

"Sounds good," Huckleberry admitted. "Beans work, too. You cut one in half, take a little blood from the wart and put it on a piece of bean. Then you bury it at a crossroads at midnight when there's no moon, and you burn the other part of the bean."

"That's true, Huck."

They parted after swapping treasures: Huck's tooth for a tick Tom had caught. Tom felt much wealthier, but he arrived at school late. When he went in he discovered his new blond beloved was sitting at a desk. Next to her was the only free seat.

"Thomas Sawyer! Why are you late again?"

"I stopped to talk to Huckleberry Finn," Tom answered, too struck by love to remember the excuse he had prepared.

"What did you say? That's the most impudent confession I've ever heard. Give me the cane."

He got a good whipping and then followed the order he had been waiting for. "Now go and sit next to the new girl."

Tom humbly sat down beside his unknown idol and pretended to stare at his book.

By and by Tom began to steal furtive glances at the girl. He put a peach in front of her, which was rejected with a sweep of the hand. On his slate he wrote, "Please take it— I got more."

The girl continued to ignore him. Then Tom began to draw on his slate, covering it with his hand so she could not see what he was doing. At first the girl refused to notice, but her curiosity grew. Finally she gave in. "Let me see."

And when Tom revealed his poorly drawn caricature of a house she whispered, "It's ever so nice. I wish I knew how to draw like that!"

"I'll learn you at lunchtime. It's easy. What's your name?"

"Becky Thatcher. And you're Thomas Sawyer."

"I'm Thomas when I'm bad and Tom when I'm good. Call me Tom."

Becky nodded and Tom wrote something on his slate, covering it. Becky wanted to know what it was. She took Tom's hand and tried to move it. Tom pretended to resist but let his hand slip little by little until three words were uncovered: "I love you."

"You bad thing!" Becky gave his hand a smart rap, but she reddened and looked pleased.

Just then the teacher's strong fingers closed on Tom's ear, ending his game. But though his ear tingled, his heart was jubilant.

That night a loud meow got Tom out of his bed. It was Huck Finn's signal.

Tom climbed out the window, gave an answering meow, crept to the roof of the woodshed, and jumped down. Tom and Huck decided to test their courage in the cemetery by hiding near a fresh grave and waiting for devils to appear.

The cemetery was always full of ghosts and lost souls, and the boys were already silent

with fear when they heard some voices—it was three devils!

They began to pray when Huck saw it wasn't devils after all, but humans. Amazed, Tom and Huck watched a drunken Muff Potter and Injun Joe, accompanied by young Doctor Robinson, digging up the coffin from the new grave. They got the body out.

"We've finished now, Sawbones," Muff said. "If you don't give us five dollars he stays where he is."

"But I already paid you!" the doctor exclaimed.

A good fight got started and Doctor Robinson knocked Muff out with a blow and Injun Joe stuck Muff's big knife into the doctor's body and then put it in Muff's hand.

When Muff woke up, Joe convinced the drunken man that he had killed Doctor Robinson without realizing it, but that Joe would keep his secret.

Tom and Huck fled into town, speechless with terror. Finally Huck spoke. "If we tell and Injun Joe doesn't hang, he'll kill us. We got to keep mum. Injun Joe wouldn't make anymore of drowning us than a couple of cats." They made a blood pact.

Vacation time was coming, and the students were anxiously awaiting it. At recess Tom found Becky in the classroom looking at an anatomy book belonging to their teacher. Startled, Becky accidentally ripped one of the pages.

When class began again, the teacher demanded furiously "Who tore my book?" No one spoke, so he went down the list of students. "Was it you, Benjamin Rogers? You, Joe Harper? . . ."

The answers were all, "No, sir." But Tom looked at Becky's pale face and knew she could not lie. He trembled for her.

"Rebecca Thatcher, was it you?"

An idea flashed into Tom's brain and standing up he shouted, "I done it!"

The adoration that shone in Becky's eyes was compensation enough for the whipping he was going to get.

During vacation the trial of Muff Potter began. Muff had been accused of killing Doctor Robinson and all the evidence was against him. Tom and Huck knew he was innocent and their consciences troubled them. In court the real murderer, Injun Joe, testified against Muff. When Tom was called as a witness, he decided to tell the truth. He described what he had seen in the cemetery, and just as he came to the part with Injun Joe and the knife there came a crash. Quick as lightning Injun Joe jumped out a window and was gone. Muff was declared innocent and Tom became the town hero.

When the new school year began, Tom and Huck found a new obsession: hunting for treasure. On one of their expeditions they discovered that Injun Joe was still in town, disguised as a deaf-mute Spaniard, and that he had found a chest full of old gold coins that he planned to share with an accomplice.

A school outing was organized. The whole class went into a cave by the river, but Tom and Becky got separated from the group when Tom, showing off for Becky, found a natural stairway for them to explore. At first they made smoke-marks with their candles to trace their way back, but a group of bats scared them into running deeper into the cave. Suddenly they realized they were lost. Becky became frightened and Tom tried to calm her, sure that he could find his way.

But the candles they were carrying began to burn down and Tom kept getting confused. Finally the candles went out. They found themselves in the dark, wandering around hopelessly, hand in hand.

Tom went a little bit ahead and saw a human hand, holding a candle, appearing behind a rock. Tom gave a relieved shout until he saw the figure emerge—it was Injun Joe! But Joe ran off, not recognizing Tom's voice, and soon a search party that had been formed found the two missing children. Aunt Polly, Becky's parents, and the whole town rejoiced.

About two weeks later, Tom learned that Becky's father had put up a locked iron door at the cave's entrance so no one would ever get lost in there again.

Tom turned white as a sheet. "Injun Joe's in there!" he exclaimed.

Within a few minutes the news had spread and a dozen boats were on their way to the riverside cave. When the cave door was unlocked they saw Injun Joe, dead, with a broken knife by his side, and his face against the crack under the door, as if his eyes had been searching for light and freedom to the very end. Tom felt pity for poor Joe but also immense relief.

Huck and Tom remembered that Injun Joe had discovered treasure, and they decided to look for it in the cave. Finally they found it!

They split the money. Huckleberry Finn was no longer poor. A widow took care of him, making him wash every day. He even had to eat with a knife and fork! He was hurled into society and his sufferings were almost more than he could bear.

"The thing ain't working, Tom. The widow won't let me sleep in the woodshed, and I got to wear them clothes that just smothers me. And grub comes too easily. Looky-here, Tom, being rich ain't what it's cracked up to be. Everything's so awful regular I can't stand it."

"Well, everybody lives that way, Huck. Besides, I can't let you into my gang of robbers if you ain't respectable."

"All right, Tom. I'll try it for a month."

"We'll meet at midnight, swear on a coffin, and sign it in blood."

"Now that's something I like!" said Huck. "It's a million times bullier than pirating. The widow will be proud of me, I'll become such a rippin' robber!"

What came afterward does not form a part of this chronicle, which is the story of a boy and thus will have to end here so as not to turn into the story of a man.

Herman Melville

Herman Melville was an American novelist, poet, and essayist. During his lifetime his early novels were popular, but by the time of his death he had been forgotten as a writer. In fact, *Moby-Dick*, considered a failure while Melville was alive, was partly responsible for his drop in recognition. The novel was "rediscovered" in the twentieth century and is now considered a literary masterpiece.

Melville was born in New York and went to sea as a cabin boy when he was nineteen. His first trip was to England. Later he sailed on a whaling ship bound for the South Pacific (he drew on his experiences from this journey to write *Moby-Dick*). He lived among natives in the *Marquesas* Islands and was imprisoned in Papeete, Tahiti. Novels such as *Typee, Omoo, Mardi, Redburn,* and *White-Jacket* depict the life of the sailor. One of Melville's most important works was the short story "Bartleby the Scrivener."

Following scathing reviews of his novel *Pierre*, publishers became wary of Melville's work. He turned to poetry but found that his verse was not appreciated either. He died in obscurity in New York City.

MOBY-DICK

Queequeg

Call me Ishmael. Some years ago, when I was a young man who lived in the city and taught school, I yearned to go to sea. I wanted to see Cape Horn and the Pacific and to travel on an exciting whaling expedition. One cold Saturday in December I arrived in New Bedford on my way to Nantucket, where the whaling ships docked. But the little steamer that went to Nantucket had already left, so I had to spend two nights waiting in New Bedford. Having little money, I needed cheap lodgings. I found an inn where I had to share a bed with another sailor, a harpooner also looking to set out on an ocean adventure.

I didn't want to go to bed until the harpooner came, but it got very late and he still did not appear. As I began to fall asleep I heard strong footsteps and a ray of light shone under the door. The door opened and—my God! I was horrified by the sight of his face, which was yellow and purple, as if covered in bruises. On closer inspection I realized that his face was tattooed. The man's skull was shaved except for a kind of braided topknot on his forehead. He undressed, approached the table, and took up what looked to me like a tomahawk and, putting the end of the handle in his mouth, lit the other end, blowing out enormous clouds of smoke.

When he found me in his bed, he was not pleased, but the inn's landlord straightened things out and when we woke up the next morning, we quickly became good friends. The harpooner's name was Queequeg.

The Pequod

It turned out that Queequeg was the son of the king of a place called Kovoko, a far away island not located on any map. Queequeg and I decided to go to sea together. It was my job to find a whaling ship we could join. I walked around the port until I found the *Pequod*, an impressive, noble, old ship that had sailed all four oceans through rough seas and typhoons.

I went up to the deck to sign up to join the *Pequod* crew. There I saw a muscular old man, dark from years of sunburn.

"Are you the captain of the *Pequod*?" I asked.

"Suppose I am," he growled. "What do you want?"

"To sail."

He looked me up and down. "You don't know anything about whales, do you?"

"Nothing, but I'll learn fast."

"Really?" He stared me in the eye, took a step closer, and said in a low voice, "Have you seen Captain Ahab?"

"Oh," I said, embarrassed. "I thought you were the captain."

"I'm Peleg, young man. I'm in charge of hiring the crew here. But if you really want to know what whale hunting is like, I recommend you take a look at Captain Ahab. He's a grand, ungodly man, who only has one leg. The other one was eaten, chopped to bits by the most monstrous whale that's ever existed. Do you still want to sail with us?"

I could tell Peleg meant to scare me. But I was determined to join the crew and go to sea with this great ship. "Yes, sir," I said proudly.

"Well, consider yourself signed on," he said to my relief. Then I remembered about Queequeg.

"Peleg," I said, "I have a friend who would also like to sail and who has killed more whales than I could count."

"Bring him along," said Peleg. "We sail at six o'clock tomorrow morning."

It was very cold and foggy the next morning, and still dark, when Queequeg and I went down to the port and stepped on board the *Pequod*. On the ship everything was eerily silent.

When the sun came up, we could see who were to be our companions for the next three years of sailing, storms, and whale hunts. "Have you signed on?" the first mate, Starbuck, asked us.

"Yes," we told him.

"We're out to sea today," he continued. "The captain came last night."

"Captain Ahab?" I asked.

"Who else?"

We set sail and were soon on the high seas. But for days and days no one on board saw Captain Ahab.

Captain Ahab

One gray morning, with a strong wind filling the *Pequod's* sails, I went on deck for the morning watch. When I glanced over at the ship's bow, I suddenly felt a chill. There, standing alone, was the fierce figure of Captain Ahab.

He looked like a man that someone had pulled out of the fire. A vivid scar ran all the way across his face, the scar that sailors told me he received from a thunderbolt. He had a rigid posture, probably from resting on that leg of ivory I heard that the crew made for him out of the jaw of a sperm whale. From that morning on, the regular click of his ivory heel was to be heard every day as he anxiously paced across the quarterdeck.

"All hands astern!" he ordered one day, wanting to see all the men at once. This was a very unusual command.

When the crew was gathered, he began, "All of you have heard me speak of a white whale." He reached into his pocket and held out his fist, slowly opening it. Gold sparkled in the sunlight. "Look what I have here. It's a Spanish gold coin. It's worth sixteen dollars, boys. Whoever spies the whale will receive this coin as a reward. Keep your eyes wide open, lookouts!" Ahab nailed the gold coin to the mast.

"Hurrah!" shouted the sailors.

"Captain Ahab," Starbuck asked, "is that white whale of yours the one some call Moby-Dick?"

The captain's face lit up with pain. "Moby-Dick!" he cried. "Do you know that whale?"

"Doesn't he move his tail in a strange way, like a fan? And doesn't he have many harpoons stuck in his skin, twisted like—"

"Like corkscrews, yes!" shouted Ahab. "Those are my harpoons—by all the devils in hell! The whale you saw is Moby-Dick. And I want him! It was him that disfigured me and to Moby-Dick I owe this leg of bone I'm leaning on now."

Starbuck looked unconvinced, so Ahab continued, "I seek out Moby-Dick to avenge myself of all the wrongs in the world. I am a prisoner and how can a prisoner reach outside except by thrusting through the wall? To me, the white whale is that wall!"

"May God help us!" murmured a sailor in a low voice.

Starbuck, the first mate, tried to remind the captain that the *Pequod* was supposed to be hunting many whales in order to bring back as much of their oil as possible to businesses back home that would buy it. He worried that looking for just one whale would be distracting and keep the crew from getting home on schedule. But Ahab's hunger for revenge against Moby-Dick was an obsession. The hunt for this one whale was now to be our only mission.

Days passed, then weeks, and months. The *Pequod* sailed into the Cape of Good Hope. Meanwhile, I was learning how to be a whaler. There was such a thrill when, after nights of silence, the lookout up high on the mast would suddenly see a little spout of water shooting up over the waves and shout: "Thar she blows! Thar she blows!" I watched with excitement when the boats went down and the hunt would begin.

But the one whale that mattered, the one called Moby-Dick, still failed to appear. Near Java we thought we sighted him, but it was just a giant squid. When other ships crossed our path, their captains would come aboard and provide news from home. But all Ahab would ask was, "Have you seen the white whale?"

I became very sad when my friend Queequeg, so big and strong, became violently ill with fever. It was the custom among seamen that when one of the crew died he was thrown into the sea, wrapped in his hammock. Queequeg was frightened his body would be eaten by sharks, so he asked the ship's carpenter to make him a thick coffin. The coffin was made, but then Queequeg's health improved. He amazingly recovered and used the coffin as his storage chest.

The White Whale

The whaling season was nearing its end and still no one had seen Moby-Dick. One night, after a violent typhoon, Captain Ahab came out of his cabin. The ghostly light of Saint Elmo's Fire glowed at the tops of the masts.

"Look!" shouted the sailors.

"Aye, lads," Ahab said. "Look at that flame. It lights the course to the white whale. He'll soon be ours!"

We came at last to the South Pacific Ocean. We were about to set course for the earth's equator when we were awakened one night by the voice of the lookout.

"Thar she blows! Thar she blows! With a hump like a snow hill—it's Moby-Dick!" His whiteness was terrifying.

Every man on deck ran to get a look at the famous whale. They launched the whaleboats, and the harpooners sharpened their deadly irons. The oarsmen bent their backs to fight the power of the waves.

Captain Ahab, even with his ivory leg, climbed down to one of the little boats himself and commanded the oarsman from the back. "Row!" he shouted. "Fall upon the whale. Leeward, leeward! The gold coin is mine!"

"It's jumping there!" a man cried. And we could see the white whale leaping straight up as if he were as light as a salmon.

"Do you see it now?" Ahab asked.

But the white whale disappeared as quickly as he came.

"Nothing, sir," we said.

Then all the water around us slowly began to rise and slide down, as if a mountain of ice were coming up out of the sea. All the men held their breath and then a monstrous shape sprung out of the sea, covered with tangled ropes and riddled with harpoons. He hung for an instant in the air, his whiteness glaring in the foggy mist, and then fell heavily, crashing into the waves.

Moby-Dick seemed possessed by all the demons of hell.

"Onward!" Ahab shouted to the oarsmen, and the harpoonists flung their iron spears at the massive white body.

When the boat got very close, the old captain arched his back and threw his own harpoon deep into the flesh of the animal who had taken his leg so long ago. Moby-Dick twisted the long length of his body and knocked three oarsmen from the boat. At the same time, turning with great speed, he threw himself forward into the *Pequod* itself.

"The ship!" the oarsmen shouted.

But it was too late. The *Pequod* had taken too great a hit and began to sink, leaving a whirlpool behind it.

In their rush to save the ship, the crew did not notice that Captain Ahab had gotten entangled in the rope from his harpoon, which was still planted in the whale. As Moby-Dick swam away, the rope slipped around Ahab's neck, pulled him from the boat, and dragged the captain out to sea along with the whale.

Only I escaped alive from that terrible adventure. I would have drowned if I had not seen Queequeg's coffin, which I grabbed onto to keep me afloat in the rough waters. It was my lifeboat until I was rescued at last by a passing ship.

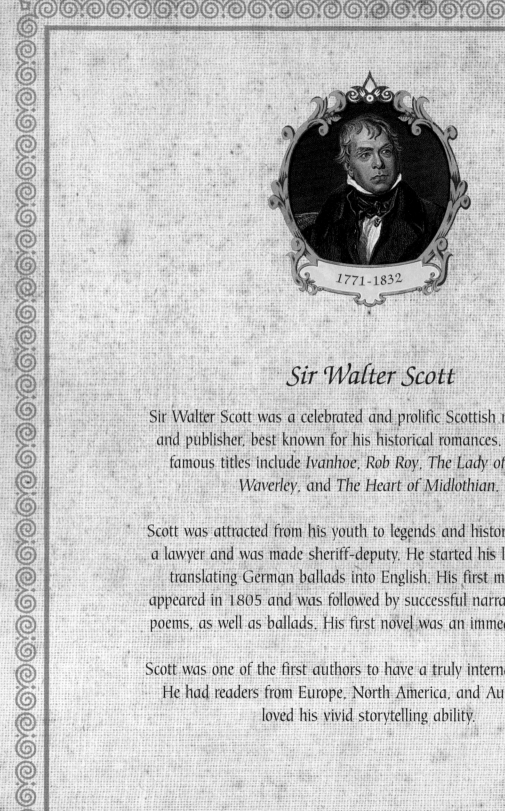

1771-1832

Sir Walter Scott

Sir Walter Scott was a celebrated and prolific Scottish novelist, poet, and publisher, best known for his historical romances. Some of his famous titles include *Ivanhoe*, *Rob Roy*, *The Lady of the Lake*, *Waverley*, and *The Heart of Midlothian*.

Scott was attracted from his youth to legends and history. He became a lawyer and was made sheriff-deputy. He started his literary career translating German ballads into English. His first major poem appeared in 1805 and was followed by successful narrative and lyric poems, as well as ballads. His first novel was an immediate success.

Scott was one of the first authors to have a truly international career. He had readers from Europe, North America, and Australia who loved his vivid storytelling ability.

IVANHOE

The Castle of Cedric the Saxon

During ancient times, in that pleasant part of merry England watered by the river Don, a huge forest covered the hills and valleys. Long years had passed since good King Richard the Lionhearted had left for the Crusades. Without the king's protection, the Norman invaders—who became the ruling class after William the Conqueror came to England in 1066—practiced all sorts of villainy against the Saxons. Prince John, Richard's brother, who hoped to seize the throne if the king did not return from the Crusades, did nothing to prevent this wrongdoing.

The sun was setting and one of Cedric the Saxon's serfs, Gurth, was herding swine, while the clown, Wamba, fixed his jester's cap with its jingling bells. They heard the thunder of horses galloping and soon found themselves surrounded by the attendants of two noble Norman warriors.

One knight asked, "Is there anywhere we could find lodging? Where is the dwelling of Cedric the Saxon?"

Gurth replied, "I know not if I should show the way to my master's house."

Wamba gave them complicated and incorrect directions, telling them to turn left at the Sunken Cross.

Gurth turned to Wamba, "If those knights follow the directions you have given them, they will not easily reach the castle tonight."

"No," replied the jester. "The castle is not a good place for them—I would not show the dog where the fox lies, if I don't want the dog to hunt him."

In the great hall of Cedric's castle, Rotherwood, dinner was being served. Servants and guests sat at tables of rough-hewn wood and serving men stood awaiting the orders of their noble lord. Cedric was still a powerful man although he had grown old, and his face showed his pride and fierceness, for he had spent his life defending his rights against the Norman invaders.

The sound of a horn and the barking of the dogs echoed through the hall.

"To the gate, rogues!" shouted Cedric.

A guard returned to announce the arrival of the two Norman knights Gurth and Wamba had encountered earlier, Aymer de Jorvaulx (known for his covetousness) and Brian de Bois-Guilbert (known for his bravery and cruelty). They requested food and lodging for themselves and their attendants.

Cedric growled, "Normans or Saxons, no one will ever have an excuse to put the hospitality of Rotherwood in doubt. Make them welcome."

As the guests came into the hall, the lovely Lady Rowena, Cedric the Saxon's ward, entered for dinner. The eyes of the newcomers were drawn to her beauty while they told of their adventures in Palestine and invited Cedric to the tournament to be held in Ashby.

A servant announced that Sir Isaac of York, a Jew, was also asking shelter for the night. He was received coldly and with contempt, and no one seemed about to make a place for him at the table, until a pilgrim sitting next to the fire, stood up and said to him, "Old man, my clothes are dry now and my hunger satisfied. You are wet and hungry."

Meanwhile, the two Norman knights continued their conversation about a tournament that had pitted six Normans against six Saxons. They praised the bravery of their people until the pilgrim interrupted, speaking passionately.

"No one could beat the Saxons, led by good King Richard. I still remember the names of four of those valiant knights that fought beside the king, though I have forgotten the fifth."

"I remember," broke in the Norman Bois-Guilbert. "Ivanhoe was the one who vanquished me, when my horse's reins broke. But I will say for all to hear that if he had the courage, and were in England, I would challenge him at next week's tournament."

"And I affirm that Ivanhoe would accept any honorable challenge," answered Lady Rowena. The pilgrim seconded this.

They all retired to bed, and when dawn was breaking the pilgrim left his humble pallet to find Isaac who was sleeping in a nearby chamber.

"Wake up! I come as your friend, for you are in danger."

"Sir, by the God of Israel, I thank you."

Isaac had reason to be frightened, since the Normans were in the habit of mistreating Jews and stripping them of all their possessions. Isaac at once followed the pilgrim who spoke to the swineherd, Gurth, and obtained some mules.

Isaac and the pilgrim left the castle using shortcuts through the woods, which the pilgrim knew very well.

They journeyed for several hours until, from the top of a hill, they could see the city of Sheffield.

"Here we must part," said the pilgrim.

"Not until I have given you something in return. I know you want a steed and armor for the tournament. In Leicester a man will provide you with them in exchange for this paper," and he handed him a document with Hebrew writing on it. The pilgrim refused the gift, but Isaac insisted and they parted.

The Tournament and the Masked Knight

King Richard had become a prisoner of the Duke of Austria and the conniving Prince John did everything he could to keep Richard imprisoned. At the tournament of Ashby, John, richly outfitted, rode proudly into the arena, turning his horse here and there and looking at the maidens who crowded the stands. Among them was the beautiful Rebecca, Sir Isaac of York's daughter. The prince marveled at her beauty and tried to get her a good seat, but the jester Wamba interfered, and Rebecca and her father were forced to sit in the lower seats.

Prince John declared, "Today's champion will be permitted to name the Queen of Beauty and of Love. Until then her throne will remain unoccupied." The heralds proclaimed the rules of the tournament:

1. The five Norman challengers, whose colors are black and red, will confront all the knights who come forward.
2. Opponents will be chosen by touching the knight's shield with the point of the lance.
3. When the knights present have crossed five lances each, Prince John will name the day's champion, who will receive a charger as his prize and will have the honor of choosing the Queen of Love and Beauty.

The knights then entered, and at the sound of trumpets, the combat began. The superior strength and skill of the Normans, led by Bois-Guilbert, brought all their opponents down into the dust.

The shouts of the crowd, the clash of arms and horses smothered the exclamations of disgust made by Cedric who, accompanied by Lady Rowena, had not wanted to miss the tournament. All the Saxon knights had been vanquished and the tournament seemed to be coming to an end when the horn sounded a challenge. An unknown masked knight rode into the arena. On his shield could be read the Spanish word, Desdichado, or "Disinherited."

The Disinherited Knight rode his black horse toward the Norman shields and with the point of his lance touched the shield of Bois-Guilbert, the toughest competitor. The fight was long and hard, and though both were hit, it was Bois-Guilbert who fell. After fighting and besting the other four Norman knights, the Disinherited Knight won the day.

When Prince John reminded the unknown knight that he had the privilege of choosing the Queen of Love and Beauty, he offered the crown to Lady Rowena, without lifting the visor of his helmet so that they could see his face. Prince John and his attendants tried to guess the knight's identity, worrying that he might be one of King Richard's men.

The next day dawned radiantly, and all made ready to watch the fighting in the general tournament. All the knights who wished to participate were divided into two groups, one under the command of Bois-Guilbert and the other under the mysterious rider, the Disinherited Knight.

With his eyes hidden by his helmet and surrounded by Norman knights, Bois-Guilbert scanned the crowd for the lovely Rebecca, for whom he had begun to feel an overwhelming passion.

There she was, but her eyes, like those of Lady Rowena, seated in the place of honor of the Queen of Love and Beauty, were only for the Disinherited Knight. The heralds gave the order for the contest to begin. The arena was soon noisy with the clash of lances and littered with broken pieces of armor. The ladies sometimes covered their faces on seeing their champion fall.

The Disinherited Knight's group was much weaker, and he found himself outnumbered. But one of his men, the Black Knight, sprang into action. Together the Black Knight and the Disinherited Knight went to work on the Normans, and when the Disinherited Knight unhorsed the weary Bois-Guilbert, the tournament came to an end.

Prince John wanted to name the Black Knight the day's champion, but he had suddenly disappeared, so John turned to the Disinherited Knight, saying, "You have the right to receive the crown of honor from the hands of the Queen of Love and Beauty." The champion bowed weakly. They had him kneel before the throne occupied by Lady Rowena and, despite his feeble protests, the marshals of the field cut off the victor's helmet.

A muffled cry and a name burst from the lips of Cedric and Lady Rowena on seeing the mysterious knight's face. "Ivanhoe!" they shouted.

For it was indeed Ivanhoe, Cedric's son who had been disinherited for going to the Holy Land with King Richard. Lady Rowena almost wept to see her beloved, but Cedric hurried to separate the two.

Then, to general alarm, the knight collapsed, and on removing his armor they could see that the point of a lance had pierced his breastplate.

Cedric wished to take care of his son who had now returned, forgetting his anger of years before. But in the confusion Ivanhoe had already been carried away and it was impossible to find him. Isaac of York, with his daughter, Rebecca, who was a skilled healer, sheltered Ivanhoe until he was better.

Captivity

But while Ivanhoe was with Isaac and Rebecca, Bois-Guilbert had decided to steal the lovely Rebecca for his bride and to steal Lady Rowena to be his friend's bride. Bois-Guilbert captured Rebecca and her father, as well as Cedric, Rowena, and their men. He imprisoned them all in his castle, shutting Rebecca up in a distant tower, while the other captives were separated and put into different rooms, except for old Isaac of York. Given his condition as a wealthy Jew, the Norman knights hoped that under torture he would reveal to them the hiding place where he kept his money. He was chained up in a horrible dungeon where iron bars awaited him, red hot from burning coals.

Cedric the Saxon, for his part, defied his proud jailors, and Lady Rowena, whose beauty had captured the heart of one of her captors, found out that her adored Ivanhoe had also been taken prisoner.

Rebecca feared for her virtue, Lady Rowena for the life of her beloved; Cedric the Saxon cursed his fate, humiliated by Norman pride, while the terrified Isaac could only await the hot iron that would burn his flesh.

Meanwhile, Wamba, the jester, escaped from Bois-Guilbert unnoticed. He made his way to the forest where the famous archer Locksley, who some called Robin Hood, and his band of men made their home. Wamba asked for their help, seeing among them the mysterious Black Knight who had attracted attention for his valor during the tournament at Ashby.

Robin Hood and his men, as well as the Black Knight, agreed to attack the Normans. The group surrounded Bois-Guilbert's castle and began the assault, their well-aimed arrows preventing the enemy soldiers from approaching the battlements.

In the heat of the battle a fire had been started, and the archers, without ceasing to fight, began freeing the captives. Thus they found Cedric and Rowena and freed Isaac from his shackles. But meanwhile, the crazed Bois-Guilbert entered the chamber where Rebecca was caring for the again wounded Ivanhoe.

"I have sworn to share everything with you," he said, "and now is the time. Come!"

The beautiful Rebecca refused, but she could do nothing against the brutality of the Norman who, grasping her arm, dragged her away, while Ivanhoe, unconscious, was unaware of what was happening.

The Norman and his prisoner escaped from the castle, whose hidden corners and secret passages Bois-Guilbert knew perfectly.

When the victorious archers reached the chamber, only Ivanhoe was to be found there, wounded and still unconscious. Rebecca had disappeared but, in spite of Isaac of York's distress, that did not cloud the joy of the Saxons. They had been victorious, and could now divide up Bois-Guilbert's wealth among themselves.

The Judgment of God

Bois-Guilbert could not force Rebecca to his will, so she was accused of witchcraft before the courts.

Witnesses were called to testify to the evil deeds of the suspected witch. To the surprise of all, Rebecca asked to be tried by the Judgment of God.

The knight Brian de Bois-Guilbert would act as the injured party and thus would fight against whoever might present himself to defend her.

Time passed and no one came forth. Rebecca's death seemed to have been decided, when suddenly hundreds of voices clamored, "A champion, a champion!" and a knight advanced toward the gallery. It was Ivanhoe. Though still suffering from his wound, he vanquished the Norman knight once again and thus forced the court to recognize that the lovely Rebecca was completely innocent.

There only remains to be added that good King Richard, who was the unknown knight in black armor that Wamba had noticed during the tournament, reigned from then on in an England that was more just, until he died.

Main Characters of the 11 Adventures

ROBINSON CRUSOE
by Daniel Defoe

Friday

Robinson Crusoe

SANDOKAN
by Emilio Salgari

Sandokan

Yáñez

Marianna

TREASURE ISLAND
by Robert Louis Stevenson

John Silver

Jim Hawkins

Ben Gunn

Magua

Cora

The hunter

The last of the Mohicans

THE ADVENTURES OF TOM SAWYER
by Mark Twain

Aunt Polly

THE LAST OF THE MOHICANS
by James Fenimore Cooper

Injun Joe

Tom

Becky

Huckleberry Finn

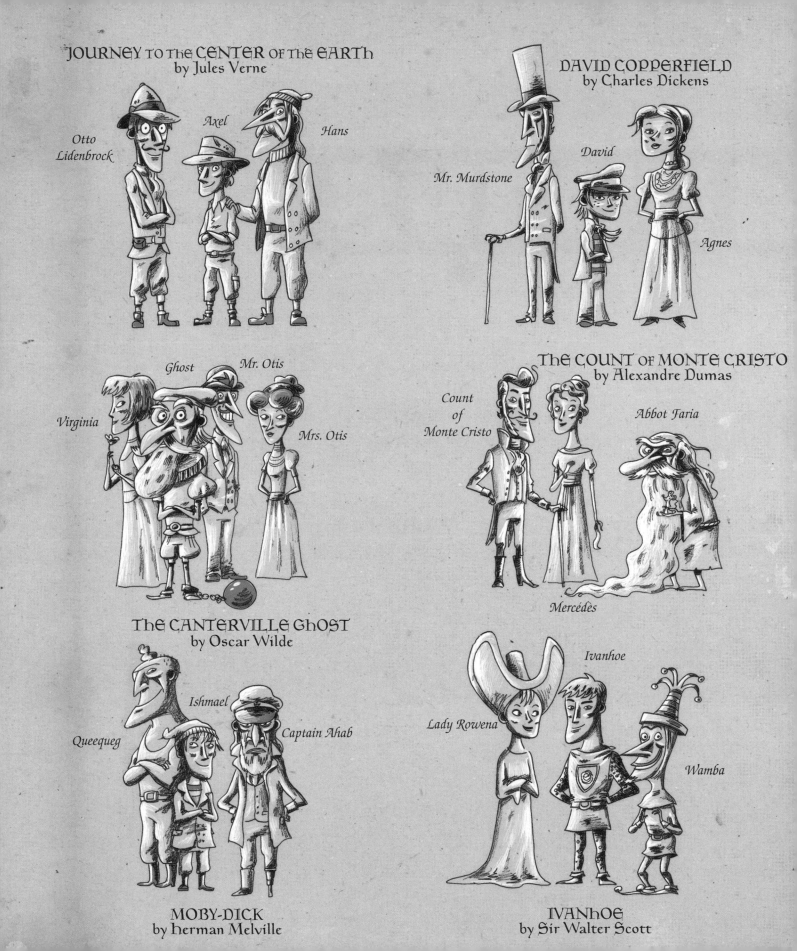

JOURNEY TO THE CENTER OF THE EARTH
by Jules Verne

Otto Lidenbrock

Axel

Hans

DAVID COPPERFIELD
by Charles Dickens

Mr. Murdstone

David

Agnes

Ghost

Mr. Otis

Virginia

Mrs. Otis

THE CANTERVILLE GHOST
by Oscar Wilde

THE COUNT OF MONTE CRISTO
by Alexandre Dumas

Count of Monte Cristo

Abbot Faria

Mercédès

Queequeg

Ishmael

Captain Ahab

MOBY-DICK
by Herman Melville

Lady Rowena

Ivanhoe

Wamba

IVANHOE
by Sir Walter Scott

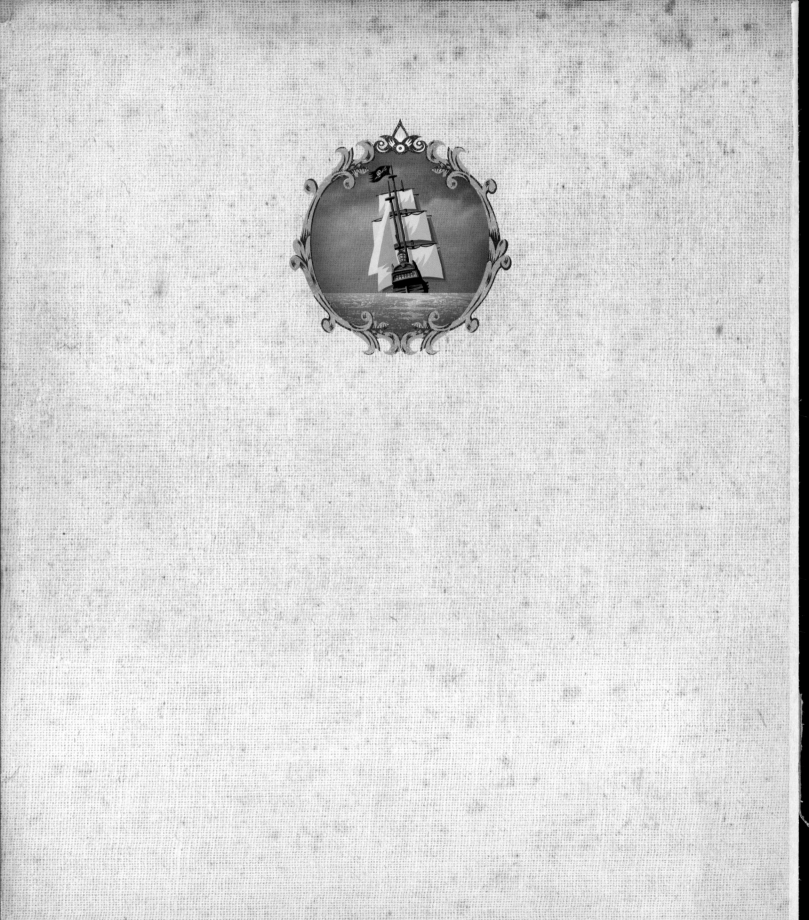